**DO NOT REMOVE
CARDS FROM POCKET**

ALLEN COUNTY PUBLIC LIBRARY

FORT WAYNE, INDIANA 46802

You may return this book to any agency, branch,
or bookmobile of the Allen County Public Library.

DEMCO

Kentucky
Daughter

Kentucky Daughter

CAROL J. SCOTT

Clarion Books

TICKNOR & FIELDS: A HOUGHTON MIFFLIN COMPANY

New York

Acknowledgments

For information about blue crabs, I would like to express my indebtedness to William W. Warner, author of *Beautiful Swimmers: Watermen, Crabs, and the Chesapeake Bay*, and to Nellie Rodgers, president of P. K. Hunt & Son, Incorporated, in Hampton, Virginia.

I also wish to express my gratitude to Doris Courtney and Debbie Woythal, weavers in Barrington, Illinois, for their contributions to my knowledge of weaving.

For editorial suggestions that improved the early drafts of this book, I would like to thank Jasmine Candlish, Linda Girard, and Marilyn Perry. Most of all, I owe a debt of gratitude to the skilled editing of James Giblin, editor and publisher of Clarion Books.

And special thanks to Jean Tolle, who gave me the idea in the first place.

Clarion Books
Ticknor & Fields, a Houghton Mifflin Company
Copyright © 1985 by Carol J. Scott

Library of Congress Cataloging in Publication Data

Scott, Carol J.
 Kentucky daughter.
Summary: Mary Fred is excited to leave her depressed mining area in Kentucky to attend a city high school in Virginia, but her experiences are not all pleasant.
 [1. High schools — Fiction. 2. Schools — Fiction]
I. Title.
PZ7.S4165Ke 1985 [Fic] 84-12737
ISBN 0-89919-330-7

S 10 9 8 7 6 5 4 3 2 1

With love and admiration
for my daughter,
Cynthia Carol Miller

Chapter 1

Soon after Mama finished baking my birthday cake, my two baby sisters came tearing through the front room and out into the kitchen. "Bushel of wheat, bushel of clover; all not hid, can't hide over!" Molly hollered.

"Hide yourselves somewhere besides this kitchen," I said, "or I'll tan your behinds!"

I chased Molly and June back into the front room. Then I leaned over and whispered into Molly's ear. "Go out to the road and check the mail for me," I said.

"No! I want to play inside with Junie."

"Shhh!" I said. "It won't take you long. I'll give you a nickel. But don't tell."

"I don't want to. I can't reach the box, anyways."

"A big first-grade girl like you? Sure you can."

"I don't want to."

"All right, then, but keep your noise out of the kitchen. I'm trying to study."

I walked to the window, pressed my forehead to the glass, and peered down the long rutted strip of dirt drive that pushes its way through the trees from our house to the road; I could barely see the mailbox at the end. Maybe the mail truck had already come.

I should have gone out earlier and put something in the box, something like one of those postage-free cards asking for more information on a correspondence course. Not that I needed any information like that, but I could have raised the red flag to signal the mailman to stop. After he picks up the mail, he always puts down the flag; then I know when he's gone by. Why hadn't I thought of that?

I went back to my books on the kitchen table.

"What're you studying, honey?" Mama asked, drying her hands on a dish towel.

My sister Cindy Lou came in and sat down across from me.

"Grammar," I said. "Mrs. Swiggett says the most important thing is to study grammar and learn to speak correct. Correctly."

"The most important thing in the *whole* world is to study grammar?!" Cindy Lou bent over laughing. "If she thinks that, she's really dumb."

"She is not. She's the best teacher in our school. And you know it, too."

"She's all right," Cindy Lou said. "But it's Saturday and your birthday to boot. I bet even Mrs. Swiggett wouldn't pore over a pile of books on her birthday."

"No sin to want to better yourself," Mama said. "But you don't need to go at it so hard on a special day like today, Mary Fred."

"All she ever does is stare at a book," Cindy Lou said. "What good's reading the Bible and Shakespeare and novels what's hundreds of pages long?"

"Mary Fred likes to learn." Mama reached over and mussed my hair.

"Maybe so," said Cindy Lou, "but I end up doing half her

chores while she's reading history books and measuring up the sides of triangles in arithmetic books. And all the blessed time she's after everbody in the house to be quiet."

I stared at Cindy Lou. "People who never read anything beautiful never learn the way the language works. Take you for an example. You don't say things correctly half the time."

"I say enough to get over what I mean."

"No, you don't. You don't know proper grammar. You mess up verbs and leave out words in sentences. You talk like a child."

"So? I'm not but thirteen. Ain't nothing for being ashamed about in how I talk, anyways."

"Girls," Mama said, "that's enough."

We hushed. For about two minutes. Cindy Lou's a phony sometimes. She takes a lot of pleasure from my interest in learning. Many nights after supper, she and Mama push me right up into the middle of the kitchen floor and make me recite whole speeches of Julius Caesar and Hamlet out of Shakespeare. Then they clap their hands and grin. And Cindy Lou's not too proud to get my help with her homework every night.

"What good's memorizing Latin verb tenses and grammar rules?" Cindy Lou asked, starting it all up again. "I don't see the point in all that mess. Who do you think you're going to be?"

"I said that's enough." That was Mama again.

"Well, she's so high and mighty —"

"Not one more word, Cindy Lou," Mama said.

I left the kitchen. In the front room, Molly and June had a puzzle spread all over the floor; neither of them even glanced at me. I looked out the window again, fuming about Cindy Lou. And the mail. Where *was* the mail truck today? Maybe

I should study just half an hour more, I thought, and then walk up to the road and check.

When I sat back down at the table, Cindy Lou was beating a fork against the plastic salt shaker, trying for the rhythm of a rock song she sang noisily and off key.

"Do you have to be so loud? I can't ever get anything done around here," I said.

At the kitchen counter, Mama eased a knife into a fresh chicken, cutting off a wing with one clean slice at the breast socket. Then she turned toward the table. "You two stop your fussing," she said, "and start on down to the store and fetch me some birthday candles now, you hear?"

"All right!" Cindy Lou jumped up from her chair. "Let's go to Lowman's! That's a treat, looking around in that store."

I sighed and closed my books. "It's two miles to Lowman's, Mama. Takes up the whole afternoon going down there and back." I was halfway ashamed of myself for arguing with someone who was going to so much trouble over me.

"I got my head set on decorating this here cake proper," Mama said. "Ain't ever day someone has a birthday and I got sugar enough for laying up a cake in three tiers. I want it looking pretty."

Cindy Lou and I set off down the drive, my sister clutching coins Mama gave her in one hand. It was uncommonly cold for April in Dowell County, Kentucky. Walking between car tracks cut into the ground, I buttoned my sweater, looked up toward the mailbox, and listened for the sound of the mail truck on the road.

Ahead of me, Cindy Lou leaned forward into the bitter wind and yanked up the hood on her old gray sweatshirt. Faded red letters marched across her back: BRONCOS — STATE CHAMPS. Daddy bought that sweatshirt back in 1981 when

4

the high school team won the 2A-division championship in football.

I stared at the faded letters moving up and down in front of me and started singing a sad song about the coal-mining life. Last July, Daddy got killed in the coal pits; after we put Daddy away, Mama sang songs like that almost all the time.

> *"Oh, come all you fellows so young and so fine*
> *Seek not your fortune in the dark dreary mine."*

Cindy Lou turned around. "Shhh! Stop singing that old ugly song."

"I like it, Cindy."

"It's depressing."

"It is not." My sister didn't have any taste in music; all she ever listened to on the radio was the station up in Lexington that played rock music day and night. I kept on singing:

> *"Oh, it's dark as a dungeon and damp as the dew*
> *Where the dangers are double and pleasures are few*
> *Where rain never falls and the sun never shines*
> *And it's dark as a dungeon way down in the mines."*

"Cut it out, will you?" Cindy Lou said. "That makes me think about Daddy. I wish them coal pits never existed."

"*Those* coal pits, Cindy. And there's no use getting started on that. If you think you're mourning over Daddy, imagine how Mama feels."

"*You're* the one started it, singing them dark, damp, dungeon blues. And *you're* the one ought to show some respect for Mama's feelings. She's making a good show of joy for your birthday. Don't seem right, you spoiling it for her with your bad mood."

"I'm not in a bad mood." That was a lie. I hummed Mama's song more quietly and started thinking about our hard times. Our mother works every minute. She makes almost all our clothes and enough quilts for all us kids to sleep under. Mama keeps up a big vegetable garden and cans beans, tomatoes, and corn. She raises a few chickens, too. Just two days back, old Mr. Hadley walked over to our place, chopped the heads off two or three chickens, and carried away one Mama gave him for his trouble. All told, Mama makes out pretty good. Still, I couldn't help but worry about the future.

Up at the road, I ran ahead of Cindy Lou. "Maybe he's already gone," I said, yanking open the rusty, dented door of the mailbox.

"The mail carrier? You been watching for the mail all morning," Cindy Lou said. "What're you looking for?"

I peeked into the box. Empty. All the same, I slid my hand across the cold metal bottom and into the back corners, just to be sure.

"What're you looking for?" Cindy Lou asked again.

I slammed the door shut. "I haven't paid any special attention to the mail. I'm just checking the box 'cause we're out here."

"You're a bad liar. You watched the road all day last Saturday, too. You went to the window about fifty times. I'm surprised you didn't stay home from school all week so you could watch ever single day."

I started down the narrow country road that winds toward the edge of town. "Let's get going."

Cindy Lou hurried to catch up with me. "Tell me what you're expecting," she persisted, tugging on the back of my sweater. "Tell me!"

"Quit being so nosey! Mama's expecting a letter, that's all."

"From who? How come I get left out of everything interesting? How come you know Mama's waiting on some letter and I don't know nothing about it?"

"She doesn't know about it, either, Cindy Lou! I'm the only one that knows—"

"*Mama's* expecting a letter and you're the only one what knows? What's going on?"

"Drop it, will you?"

"How come you're so nervous today, Mary Fred? What's wrong with you?"

"I'm not nervous! Just leave me alone." I'd really fouled it up; I shouldn't have said a word about a letter coming for Mama. How was I supposed to get Cindy Lou to keep her mouth shut without making her suspicious? She was already suspicious.

I walked faster, glaring down at the ground. Out where we live, the one-lane road isn't much more than a broad path through some pine woods, the earth packed down hard and gutted with holes. Stepping around the worst ones, I wondered if I could trust Cindy Lou to keep my secret. She's nosey, but she'd never blabbed anything I'd told her in confidence before. Besides, I sure could use her on my side if Mama got mad when the letter came. If it ever did.

I slowed down and waited for Cindy Lou to catch up again. Maybe I could just hint around and try to figure out what my sister would think of my plans.

"Don't you ever get sick of all this?" I asked when Cindy Lou came up beside me. I motioned toward the frozen landscape on either side of the road. "Don't you wish you could get away from it and be somewhere else? Have some nice things?"

"Like what?"

"Like what? Use your head, Cindy. Look at those mine owners' kids at school. They ride around in the finest automobiles, and we don't even have a car. The girls have fancy clothes and stylish hair-dos. They go to the show on Saturday nights and out on dates."

"So? Mama ain't letting a fourteen-year-old go out with no boys, anyways. You can have a date when the time comes."

"Who'd ever ask me? I'm not all that pretty and I've —"

"Mary Fred, ain't nobody in our family so good-looking as you! You should be short and pudgy as me instead of tall and slim like Daddy — then you'd have something for complaining about."

"I'm not complaining."

"You are so. You got Mama's thick red hair, too, but all you ever do is gripe." Cindy Lou fiddled with the strings to her sweatshirt's hood. "I hate my ugly thin hair!" she said suddenly. "And I need to lose about thirty pounds!"

The change in Cindy Lou's tone startled me. When I glanced sideways, I was even more surprised by the tense expression of her face. Maybe all my sour talk had upset her. "Listen," I said, "don't pay any attention to me. You were right; I'm in a bad mood today. But that's no reason for you to get down on yourself. You need to lose five pounds. That's all."

I stopped to help her untangle the strings and get her hood on right. "You know what?" I said. "Ward Greer told me he thinks you're the prettiest girl in seventh grade."

"You're kidding!" Her eyes brightened. "Don't tease me. Did he *really*?"

"Yep. He's right, too. Actually," I said as we started walking again, "we'd both look pretty fine if we had some decent clothes."

"We got decent clothes."

8

"I'm tired of homemade things. They look awful. You can tell a homemade piece every time — it's plain tacky."

"Don't talk like that. The care Mama takes, she never sewed nothing tacky in her life. And she can't help it if she ain't got money to buy lots of frills."

"I didn't say I wanted frills."

"You do, though. You want designer jeans and classy sweaters and ski jackets and such."

"I just hate how we live, that's all."

Cindy Lou frowned at me. "Nothing wrong with how we live," she said. "I wish we had a telephone and a television, though."

"Sometimes, I . . ."

"What?"

"Oh, nothing." I concentrated on the quivering noises in the thickets beyond the barbed-wire fences that lined the road; I imagined the woods full of foxes, cottontails, and raccoons, all of them friendly. Cindy Lou's old shoes, the ones I knew good and well had holes in the soles, crunched on the frozen ground beside me.

"Tell me the truth now, Mary Fred," she said. "Do you think Ward would call me? *If* we had a phone?"

"Definitely."

She grinned. Then she eyed me more closely. "What'd you start to say before?" she asked.

"Oh, I was just thinking Mama's going to have a hard time trying to make a go of it by herself."

"That ain't so. Mama's doing real good. She's a born farmer."

"A few chickens and some vegetables don't make a farm."

"She gets good money for spinning that wool Mr. Hadley lines coffins with, too."

"That strange old fogey. He's so nervous and fidgety — makes me jumpy to be around him."

"The way you're acting today, Mary Fred, you ain't got no call for talking about folks being nervous and fidgety. As for me, I like Mr. Hadley. He's good to our family. And he's a fine artist. He makes them coffins from the best pine wood."

"*Those* coffins, Cindy." I strode ahead. "I think they're spooky-looking. Anyway, people buy nice metal caskets at a funeral parlor these days. Who'd want his old homemade coffins?"

"Plenty of folks," Cindy Lou panted, catching her breath as she rushed to keep pace with me.

The road widened. For about half a mile, we walked on gravel.

"Mr. Hadley's granddaddy made them, too," Cindy Lou said. "Folks around here know the Hadley coffins are beautiful. He makes a nice bit of money selling them things."

"It's morbid. And he cheats Mama, if you ask me. She pays a pretty cent for that fine cotton sateen she puts over the wool and he barely gives her what she needs to buy it."

"That ain't so, neither," Cindy Lou said.

"What he gives her doesn't pay for all the hours she sits up nights doing the fingerwork," I insisted. "Besides, those linings are too pretty to get put away with dead people."

"Well, Mama says Mr. Hadley gives her a fair amount and she's plenty happy to have the work."

When we came to the paved road on the edge of town, we walked quickly to Lowman's, a big discount place that's half grocery and half drugstore.

For someone who doesn't care whether Mama can afford frills, Cindy Lou Pratley acts peculiar in a store. She headed straight for the magazine rack while I got the candles. When

I needed the change Mama gave her to pay for them, I found her looking through one teen magazine after another, exclaiming over the latest fashions.

"Give me the money," I said.

She handed it to me without looking up; then she pulled down one of the women's magazines. I shrugged and went to the check-out line. After I paid for the candles, I found Cindy Lou in the cosmetics section. She had to look at all the make-up, the fingernail polish — every color — and the earrings. I was just glad they didn't have record albums; we'd have been there all day.

"Come on," I said. "I want to get home."

I couldn't seem to shake my sour mood and I'd lost my nerve about confiding in Cindy Lou. From what she'd already said, I could tell she'd never see things my way, so I stayed quiet most of the way home while Cindy Lou chattered about all the things she'd seen in the store. After a while, she stopped talking, too. That didn't last long, though.

"How come you go on about Mama not doing so good?" she asked suddenly. My sister never gives up an argument. "She made a fine profit over at the art fair last fall. She sold ever last one of her little wooden dolls."

"I know that. But she didn't make what you call 'a fine profit.' She barely got —"

"Mama's hand-sewn quilts had the prettiest rickrack edging of anybody's, too, and I heard plenty of them city ladies from Rollinsboro saying so. She sold out ever single quilt, right along with the dolls."

"I told you I know all that. But she can't support four children on —"

"You act as if Mama's never going to have anything. You talk like Mama's nothing."

"Cindy Lou!" I grabbed her elbow and held it firmly. "Don't take everything I say wrong." I loosened my grip on her arm. "Please. I'm *not* criticizing Mama. I just don't want to end up like her, that's all. I want—"

"Why not? Mama's smart as a whip!"

Obviously, Cindy Lou didn't get the point. I couldn't think of any way to make my sister understand my feelings, so I decided to give up. As we approached the mailbox again, I stared up ahead of us at our place set back on the hillside among the woods. We had a few acres cleared, but our frame house wasn't much more than a shack. Rotting two-by-fours propped up the porch. Out back sat a little tarpaper shed and some hen coops.

At the mailbox, I opened the door and ran my hand inside. Still empty. I banged the door closed with my fist.

"Tell me why you're so interested in the mail," Cindy Lou said. "I'm just curious. Is it a secret between you and Mama? What letter's Mama supposed to get?"

"Cindy Lou, please keep quiet about the letter. I shouldn't have said anything to you."

We walked in silence all the way to the yard in front of the house. Then Cindy Lou darted through a bunch of chickens, jumped over three broken-down wooden steps onto the porch, and whirled around to face me. "I'm not going to keep quiet!" she yelled. "I'm going inside right now and ask Mama what's going on."

I ran up to the edge of the porch. "Come back down here into the yard! Cindy Lou!"

A smug glow covering her face, she started a little tap dance routine. She'd won. Now I had to tell her, just to keep her quiet.

"Come back down here!" I said again.

Cindy Lou didn't budge.

I went up on the porch. "All right," I said softly, glancing toward the front door, "you might as well know what's happening. If Mama ever does get that letter from Uncle Mack and Aunt Louise, I'll need you to help me convince her."

"What's a letter from Uncle Mack and Aunt Louise got to do with me convincing Mama of anything? What're you talking about?"

Out of the corner of my eye, I saw Molly watching us through the front room window. I wasn't sure how to begin. "Nothing interesting ever happens on this place," I said, keeping my voice low. "I want . . ."

"That's not true. And what's that got to do with Aunt Louise and Uncle Mack, anyways?"

"I need a chance. I want out of . . ." I stopped and just stood there.

Cindy Lou pulled the little package of candles from the brown sack and looked at them. "Get to the point," she said.

Molly had moved away from the window; afraid she'd come out any second, I kept my eyes on the front door. "I don't know how to put it," I said quietly. "I wrote Uncle Mack and Aunt Louise about three weeks ago. I'd like to —"

"What? What'd you write them for?"

I put my hand on her shoulder. "I don't even know for sure myself. I may have made a big mistake. I wanted . . ." I sighed and moved my hand. Cindy Lou wasn't going to understand.

"What?"

"Try to understand, Cindy Lou. One day Mrs. Swiggett said she wished I could go to college. She said that if I worked hard enough I might win a scholarship. She thinks I could be a good teacher."

"So? What's that got to do with Mama's letter?"

"That night I started thinking about what Mrs. Swiggett said and I couldn't go to sleep. I got out of bed and wrote Aunt Louise and Uncle Mack. I asked them if I could come to live with them in Virginia and if they'd write Mama about it. Schools—"

"You're crazy!"

"Shhh! Talk softly. Schools are better in a big city. I want to be a teacher, Cindy Lou, and I'd get a good education there. I could meet people who—"

"Mama's *never* going to let you—"

"Shhh! Be quiet!"

"Is that why you study all the time? You planned to get smarter than us and then leave here?"

"No! I didn't plan anything. Don't you see? I just wrote the letter one night and the next day I mailed it. I didn't even stop to think about it. But I want to go. At least, I *think* I do."

Cindy Lou looked down at the sagging planks on the porch and turned the candles around in her hand. "Mama's going to like these. There's three different colors . . ." She started crying. "Look," she said after a minute, "just 'cause we fight a lot, that don't mean I don't—"

"Don't be silly! It hasn't got anything to do with you, Cindy Lou!"

"Mama'd be really upset without you here," she said. "She'd miss you. And there'd be less help for her. Things'd just be worse."

"No, they wouldn't. It'd be one less mouth for Mama to feed."

My sister's tears kept falling, and then, surprise to me, I put my arms all the way around her and hugged her tight.

"You're just the finest girl, Cindy Lou," I said. "Don't fret. Aunt Louise and Uncle Mack didn't even write to Mama. Or me. They probably never will."

I hugged her again. "Stop crying now and let's get into the house."

Chapter 2

INSIDE, I felt more cheerful. Since Mama says nobody in the Pratley family has to work a lick on their birthday, I didn't help with the supper makings. Instead, I wandered in and out of the front room and kitchen, flashing around white cards I'd put words on in big black letters. I spelled the words out loud all over the house and then went into the kitchen carrying June slung up on my hip. Mama and Cindy Lou were peeling potatoes at the sink.

"Here, June," I said, setting the child right up on the kitchen table. I held a card in front of her and pointed to the letters one at a time. "Ver-bose," I said. "That means saying too many words. Say it now; say 'verbose.'"

Molly came into the kitchen and climbed up on the table next to June.

"Verboose," June said.

Mama laughed. "That child's not but four years old. You'd best be making up a card with 'J-U-N-E.' Teach her that."

"'J-U-N-E' spells 'June,'" Molly said. "I know that one! I can spell *my* name, too." She smiled at me.

"Good! Junie'll learn to spell hers in kindergarten next year. She won't need me for that." I pulled out another card. "Privy," I said to June. "It means participating in private or secret knowledge."

Cindy Lou turned from the sink and stared at me. "Did anybody get the mail today, Mama?" she asked.

Twisting sideways in my chair to avoid Cindy Lou's stare, I dropped the cards. "Say it, June," I said, leaning over to pick them up. "Say 'privy.'"

"I sent Molly out for it," Mama said to Cindy Lou. "Just a bill from the light company."

I kept my head down and picked up more cards, surprised to feel my whole body relax. Had I really wanted Uncle Mack and Aunt Louise to write Mama? What would I do if they actually wrote and said I could come to Virginia?

Stacking my cards neatly on the table, I grabbed Molly's ankle, squeezed it, and whispered to her. "Molly can't reach the mailbox. Wonder how Molly got the mail. I bet *that's* privy!"

Molly stuck out her tongue at me. "Privy's an outhouse!" she shouted in my ear.

"Don't shout."

She stuck out her tongue again. "It's an outhouse!"

"Stop it," I said. "There's no point in teaching Junie that."

"Why not?" Cindy Lou asked, staring at me again.

"Pay attention to what you're doing, Cindy Lou!" Mama said. "You're fixin' to cut yourself."

"More people around these parts know about an outhouse than about private or secret knowledge," Cindy Lou said. She whacked a peeled potato in half with a butcher knife.

"Privy! Privy! Privy!" hollered June, climbing down from the table.

I gave June a big kiss on the cheek. "See?" I said to Mama. "This girl's going to be a genius."

After Cindy Lou put the potatoes in to boil, she went back to the bedroom; a minute later we heard rock music. Mama cleaned up the sink and turned down the flame under her chicken stew. Then she sent Molly and June out to feed the chickens.

"I thought you fed them this morning," I said.

"I did." Mama grinned. "They won't be hungry for a week. I just wanted a few minutes to talk with you. Alone." Mama's grin disappeared. "Come sit in the front room with me."

"All right. Just one second." I went down the hall and knocked on the bedroom door. "Turn that down!" I yelled at Cindy Lou.

Back in the front room, I sat on the opposite end of the sofa from Mama. What did she want to talk about?

"I got a letter from your uncle this week," she said.

I froze.

"Cat got your tongue?" she asked.

"Uncle Mack?" I looked down at the floor.

"Don't play Miss Innocent, Mary Fred."

"I shouldn't have written to them without asking you," I mumbled.

"No, you shouldn't have. And you didn't show them much courtesy, neither, seeing as how they ain't been in their new place more'n two months. You barely give them time to unpack."

My stomach burned. "I never thought about that. I didn't mean to be rude."

"I'm sure you didn't. But you could use your head a little better sometimes. You agree?"

"Yes, ma'am."

"All right. I got that off my chest." She slipped her feet out of her shoes and propped them up on the coffee table. Then she pulled a white envelope out of her apron pocket and put it on her lap. "I reckon you feel life here's pretty hard," she said. "Can't say as I blame you. Most folks around here have more hard times than good. Been that way a long time."

"I know," I said, wondering why Mama didn't get right to the topic of the letter. And why hadn't she talked to me when she first got it?

"My daddy's folks come to these hills to make their living off the land," she said. "My granddaddy owned a hundred acres. He only got sixty cents an acre selling out the mineral rights."

Trying to keep my eyes off the letter, I shifted my position and pulled on a loose string on the sofa fabric. Maybe Mama'd kept quiet two or three days so she'd have time to think over whatever Uncle Mack had written.

"Don't yank on that," Mama said. "You'll unravel the whole thing. My daddy went into the coal mines to work when he was fourteen, same age you are today."

"I didn't know that." Wasn't Mama *ever* going to tell me about the letter?

"Daddy died from lung disease," Mama continued. "And your father — David's life weren't fair to him. He just spent his years trying to feed me and four younguns until that pit caved in."

I twisted a piece of my hair and bit my bottom lip. "There's no future here!" I blurted out. "You have to own a mine or be a manager for one of the companies if you ever want to have anything."

"Plenty of future here – or anywhere – for a smart girl like you. Your uncle thinks so, too." She pulled the folded sheets of paper from the envelope in her lap. "I'll read you a bit of his letter."

I tugged at the loose string again and then remembered Mama said for me to quit. Was Uncle Mack going to say I could come?

Mama took her feet off the coffee table and tucked them up underneath her. "I got three pages here from Mack. I'll skip over to the part what has to do with what we're talking on." She ran her eyes halfway down the second page and then began to read aloud:

> "I reckon life's what you make of it most anyplace. All the same, there's not much around there but the mines for folks without an education. Lord knows our old man tried to get me and David to train for some kind of work out of the coal pits. I wish to heaven we'd listened to him, but my brother and I went from high school straight into those pits, chasing easy money. Turned out there wasn't all that much money and there was nothing easy about getting it. David gave his life for his and none of us'll ever be the same again because of that."

Mama stopped and wiped her eyes with a corner of her apron. "Reckon I'll ever stop spilling these tears?"

"After enough time passes, Mama. Someday you'll think of all the good times you and Daddy had and you'll smile."

She sat quietly a minute. Then she reached over and patted my knee. "Let's get back to this letter." She picked it up and started again:

20

"Mary Fred's a bright girl, Becky — been brighter'n blazes since she was a little thing. Many's the day David came into those mines talking about that child. He had high hopes for her and I can see why. She wrote me and Louise the finest, most intelligent letter. She says her dream is to get a good education so she can teach kids right there in Dowell County and turn their heads towards something other than the mines.

"I'd like to see Mary Fred in the schools here. She's got the brains to make something special of her life and it'd be a shame for that to be wasted. Education here *is* better. I've talked to some people in the school system since Mary Fred's letter came. They pay teachers more here, so they're able to hire some of the best people. There are special honors classes for the bright kids. The library at Hampton Junior High School's got twice as many books, magazines, and journals as the one at the community *college* back home! And they've got films, slides, videotapes, and computer terminals — all the kids are being taught something about computers in one class or another. Dowell County just can't afford that sort of thing.

"I think David would have liked to see — "

Mama turned the letter face down on the coffee table as Molly and June came in the back door and on into the front room.

"Y'all hang up your sweaters and pick up these puzzle pieces what's all over the floor here," Mama said to them.

They pulled off their sweaters, dropped them on the floor, and started tossing puzzle pieces into the box. While Mama got down on her knees and helped them, I stared at the letter on the coffee table. Uncle Mack understood! I probably shouldn't have wondered whether he would. He and Aunt Louise knew what things were like here.

When Daddy died, Uncle Mack grieved nearly as much as Mama. He changed overnight; the big, jolly man who'd had something to laugh about all the time lost twenty pounds or more and didn't smile or laugh for months. Aunt Louise took it hard, too. And, up at our house after the funeral, she ended coal mining for her husband once and for all: "You set foot in that pit once more, Mack Pratley," she said, "and you better not try setting your foot inside my door."

Uncle Mack sat silent, his head in his hands. A month later, a friend told him about jobs for welders at a big shipbuilding company on the east coast of Virginia. He went for six months to a welding school in Rollinsboro and then he and Aunt Louise moved to Virginia.

"Good job," Mama said to the little girls. "Now hang up them sweaters and go set the table for me."

Molly and June ran to the kitchen, leaving the sweaters on the floor.

Mama picked up the letter and sat back down on the sofa. "There's just a little more of this. Maybe I can finish without getting interrupted again. Here's the last part:

"I think David would have liked to see Mary Fred have this chance. I don't mean to pressure you, Becky. It's a big decision and it's yours alone to make. But David's kids are all I've got left of my brother — it'd mean the world to me to think I had something to offer any of those younguns. There are loans for college tuition and Mary Fred's probably smart enough to win a scholarship. And you know I'll help that girl. She's got a dream worth going for. If she could go back to Dowell County as a teacher, I'd feel pride in having sent something fine home to those Kentucky hills.

"Louise and I have talked this over and we both feel positive about the idea. She'll be writing you, too. It'd be a pleasure to have Mary Fred with us. We'd try hard to do right by her — you know we don't have experience being parents, but I'm hoping that love and common sense'd take care of it."

Mama folded the letter and put it back in the envelope. "Going over to Virginia might be a big chance for you," she said.

I clenched my hands in my lap. Did I want her to say I could go?

She turned around on the sofa so that she faced me. "I had big plans for getting out of here," she said. Her eyes brightened as if she was amused at herself.

"You did? Honest?"

"Sure. Before me, nobody in my family ever finished high school. I went over to Rollinsboro, waited tables ever night for a year and finished up a bookkeeping course. Got a job in the payroll department for one of the mines here. That's where I met your daddy. He come in cussin' and carrying on 'cause somebody fouled up one of his paychecks. Blessed me out in front of everbody in the office."

"That sounds just like Daddy. See, that's a memory to smile about. How come you never told me that story?"

"Subject never come up, I reckon. I planned on saving what part of my money I didn't give my folks and going to a nursing school someday. Meeting your daddy changed all that."

Mama walked over to pick up the sweaters. "Chance to get away from here don't come too often," she said. "I married David when I weren't but twenty. Twenty's an old maid for these parts, though." She smiled at me. "The next year, you was born. I didn't go back to work no more. So, here we are today and I'm a widow with four younguns."

"I'm sorry, Mama."

"Hey, don't *you* go spilling tears now." She went to the front closet and hung up the sweaters. Then she came back to me. "I ain't one bit sorry for none of my choices. I ought to think more about the good times, like you said." She leaned over and kissed my cheek. "Had myself fourteen good years with a lively, handsome man, best man ever lived. And four beautiful daughters thrown into the bargain. Got no regrets for myself, but..."

"But what?"

Mama sighed. "Ain't a daddy or a mama in the world don't want to see things a bit easier for their own kids. I just might be letting you go on over to Virginia." She put on her shoes and walked toward the kitchen. "We'll see," she said.

I stayed on the sofa by myself. "We'll see," Mama'd said! What if she ended up saying "yes"? Did I *want* to go? Wouldn't I be scared to death in a big city school full of strangers? And suppose Aunt Louise and Uncle Mack didn't like me so much when they lived with me every day? Suppose I didn't like them? Everything had seemed so simple when I wrote that letter, but now I wondered if I'd be happy living away from Mama and my sisters. And I'd miss my friends so much!

I stretched out on the sofa and closed my eyes. Why had I come up with such a dumb idea? I'd let everything Mrs. Swiggett said about me being smart go right to my head. Still, I thought I *could* do good in college and I knew Uncle Mack was right: "There's not much around there but the mines for folks without an education." I was proud of Mama for working so hard and never giving up, but Mama's life was *too* hard. There had to be a better way to live.

Restless, I sat up again. With a good education, I could come back and teach kids here. I loved Kentucky. But even if

24

I knew I'd be coming home later, did I have the nerve to leave Kentucky now?

A little later, Cindy Lou and Mama put out a supper of stewed chicken and mashed potatoes. For all of that evening, the grieving over Daddy left Mama's face. After we ate, she brought out her cake and, smiling at all her daughters, set it in the middle of the table. Even with no icing, Mama's yellow cake, three layers tall and covered with the pretty candles, was a special treat. Mama's eyes shone all through the singing of "Happy Birthday."

Before I blew out my candles, I sat still a long time with my eyes squeezed shut for making my special, private wish. I had to decide fast what I really thought about Virginia. I took a deep breath and blew hard: I wanted to go. Every single candle went out.

Mama got up and went to the back bedroom. She came out with a big box wrapped in white butcher paper covered with pictures of pretty girls I figured she'd cut from a magazine and glued onto the paper. "Happy birthday," she said, handing me the present.

I opened the box fast and pulled out a wool coat. Yellow, orange, and green-gray stripes ran lengthwise and full, loose sleeves flared out and then narrowed into knitted cuffs at the wrists.

"Oh!" Cindy Lou squealed. "You've been weaving, Mama! That's the prettiest coat I ever seen in all my born days!"

June and Molly clapped their hands.

"How'd you do that, Mama, without us knowing?" Cindy Lou asked.

"That weren't hard, you gone all day to school. I set up Mr. Hadley's loom at his place and took June down there most ever morning so's I could weave. Mr. Hadley give me so much wool that coat might as well be from him. The only hard part was keeping June from telling."

"It's a privy," said June and they all laughed.

"Where'd Mr. Hadley get that wool?" Molly asked.

"From his sheep," Cindy Lou said.

Molly's eyes widened. "He's got yellow and orange and green sheeps?"

"No, stupid," Cindy Lou said. "Mama dyed the wool."

I ran my fingers over the fabric. It felt coarse and prickly.

"It's a little itchy, honey," Mama said. "I'm sorry about that. Mr. Hadley's sheep are raised for mutton. You can't shear off no high-class wool from sheep like that. I took the stomach and back wool what's longest but even that ain't but so soft."

Mama was right. I tried not to frown as I ran my hands across the coat again. The kinkiness of the wool scratched my fingers.

Cindy Lou leaned over and turned back the lining of the coat. "Oooh, that's so soft," she said. "Feel how soft that is, Mary Fred. Isn't it nice?"

It'd be nice, all right, I thought, if all you wanted was to rub something soft for all eternity after you were dead and buried. The coat was lined with white cotton sateen, the same stuff Mama used to line Mr. Hadley's caskets! I couldn't believe my eyes. It was too morbid for words!

"Well, honey," Mama said to me, "put it on and turn around so we can see how you look in it."

I didn't need a mirror to know how I'd look. Everybody at school would stare at me wearing those loud, gaudy colors. I'd feel like a walking Christmas tree, all lit up. And it'd be even worse because the yellow and orange clashed with my red hair. I thought of the soft, subdued colors, the pale blues and grays of the ski jackets some of the girls at school wore. Maybe Cindy Lou didn't want a ski jacket, but I did.

I twirled round and round on the kitchen floor, careful not to focus my eyes on Mama's face. I didn't want her to read my feelings; I didn't want to hurt Mama. But I didn't like the loose-fitting coat with the blousy, full sleeves and those stripes going up and down. I knew how huge and tall I must look in it — just like a beanpole. That's just what I needed — something to make me look even taller when I was already nearly the tallest girl in my class and every single boy was shorter than me.

"I think it turned out halfway decent," Mama said as I kept turning.

"It's perfect!" Cindy Lou said. "Wait'll all the kids see you in that, Mary Fred!"

"She's drop dead good-looking, ain't she?" Mama said and Molly and June clapped their hands again.

Maybe some of the kids *here* would like the coat, I thought, but I was sure of one thing: kids in a big city school would die laughing at a coat like this. If I got to go to Virginia, I'd never wear it.

I stopped twirling; I was getting dizzy. I walked around the table quickly and gave Mama a kiss. "Thank you," I said. "It fits perfectly." That wasn't true, but I couldn't think of a single nice thing to say about the coat. I felt like the meanest daughter in the world.

Chapter 3

Aunt Louise and Uncle Mack wrote us many letters. Mama decided I could go, but she made me stay in Kentucky the whole summer; she didn't let me leave until the day before school started in Virginia.

Early in the morning on the last day of August, Mr. Hadley came over to drive us to the bus station in Tyler. Instead of the overalls and work shirt he always wore for everyday, he came dressed in his cheap seersucker suit, the one he wore every Sunday when we all went to church together; it was faded blue, the same color as his eyes. Mama had on her Sunday dress and my sisters wore skirts and blouses that were school clothes.

We all followed Mr. Hadley as he carried my one big suitcase out to his old brown Ford. The weight of it really slowed him down; a normal gait for Mr. Hadley was closer to a trot than a walk.

"Why's everyone dressed up?" I asked Mama. "You told me to wear these jeans."

"You'll want to be comfortable, honey, riding on that bus thirteen hours."

"The rest of us is dressed up 'cause this is a special occasion,"

Cindy Lou said, poking my ribs with her elbow. "We're getting rid of *you*!"

"Very funny," I said.

Behind his car, Mr. Hadley bent over the lock to the trunk, twisting the key hard. "Trunk lid's rusted out so bad I'll be needing a screwdriver to open it first thing you know," he said.

The lid finally sprang open. Mr. Hadley's face reddened as he struggled to lift the suitcase into the trunk. He was tall and broad-shouldered, but probably not as strong as he looked; his arms were skinny and his chest was practically caved in — besides, he was really old.

Cindy Lou and Molly and I climbed into the back seat. Mama put Junie up front with her and Mr. Hadley. After he wiped the sweat from his cheeks and nose with a handkerchief, he ran both hands through his thin white hair, pushing it up off his forehead. Then he started the car and it bounced off down the dirt drive.

"Quite a vehicle I got here," he said, shifting up into second gear. He drove like he walked and talked: lightnin' fast. "That racket is the doors rattling — bottoms of 'em's rusted out," he shouted over the noise of the exhaust. "Muffler's rusted out, too. Nothing but rust and rattles, me and this old buggy. Engine in this thing just won't die, though. This baby'll be runnin' strong when I'm a hundred."

I wondered how long that'd be. Mr. Hadley was probably ninety if he was a day.

Cindy Lou and Molly and I bounced up and down on the back seat all the way to town. At the bus station, Mr. Hadley parked on the street out front. "Wait while I go around," he said to Mama. "Door handle on your side broke this week. Door won't open from the inside."

After Mama and Mr. Hadley got my ticket, we went outside to the back of the building. The bus was already in its lane. Mr. Hadley helped the driver load my suitcase into the luggage compartment. Then he reached into the inside pocket of his suit and pulled out a green paper sack, stapled closed at the top.

"Got you a little present, Mary Fred," he said, his small blue eyes darting from my face to the bus and back as he handed it to me. "Something to keep you reading so the time'll go by fast. It'll have you hanging on every word, turning the pages in suspense." His eyes sparkled. "Don't open it 'til you get on the bus."

I nodded, surprised and pleased. As Cindy Lou looked right at me, I felt uncomfortable about the mean things I'd said about Mr. Hadley. I tapped the paper sack lightly and nodded at him again. "Thanks a lot," I said.

"Well, you knock 'em dead over in the big city, you hear?" He hesitated and then held out his hand to shake mine. "Be seeing you," he said and bolted back into the bus station.

When Molly and June reached up to me for their goodbye kisses, Cindy Lou broke down and started crying. She took Molly and June by the hand, one on each side of her, leaned over to kiss me quickly on the cheek, and turned toward the building. "Bye, Mary Fred," she said over her shoulder, walking fast.

Mama and I didn't shed any tears. After a young couple with a little boy climbed onto the bus, Mama handed my ticket to the driver who still stood beside the door. Then she hugged me tight and gave me one long last look. "Better get going," she said, slapping me on the behind.

Soon after the bus pulled out of the station, I tore open the green bag Mr. Hadley had given me. Inside was a package of chewing gum and a paperback dictionary. I didn't exactly turn the pages in suspense, but I spent the whole day with the dictionary gripped in my hands. If I wasn't staring out the window at new and strange landscapes, I was studying new and strange words – "hanging on every word," just like Mr. Hadley had said.

Thirteen hours later, my aunt and uncle met me at the bus station in Hampton. When I stepped off the bus, I spotted them right away, standing in a group of people on the pavement. Over six feet tall and wearing a bright yellow shirt, Uncle Mack stood out in the crowd. He worked his way through the people, picked me right up off the pavement, and whirled me around. "Hey, girl," he grinned, setting me down, "you're looking great!"

"So are you," I said. He'd gained back a lot of weight in the six months since I'd seen him. He was huge.

Aunt Louise stepped up and grabbed my arm. "Hi, honey. You have a good trip?"

"Yes, ma'am," I said, reaching up to give her sharp, bony shoulder a squeeze. Aunt Louise is nearly as tall as Uncle Mack and she's the skinniest person I've ever seen.

Uncle Mack got my bag and we went to his white Chevy pickup truck in the parking lot. He put my suitcase on the bed of the truck and got behind the wheel in the cab. Aunt Louise and I squeezed into the passenger seat.

"Brought you a bite to eat," Aunt Louise said, giving me a sandwich wrapped in aluminum foil. "Figured you'd be famished by now. It's just peanut butter." She reached into the glove compartment and handed me a pint carton of chocolate milk, still cold.

"Great!" I said. While I ate the sandwich, I tried to concentrate on the lights, noise, and traffic of the city around me, but most of my attention went to answering a hundred questions Aunt Louise and Uncle Mack asked about everybody in Kentucky. I didn't have time to ask them a single thing about all I saw as we drove through Hampton. In fifteen minutes we were in a residential area without many streetlights and I could hardly see anything.

"There's Hampton Junior High School up on the right," Uncle Mack said. "This is Fifth Street. We live at the end."

"It's a real nice school. Only about ten years old," said Aunt Louise.

I leaned across her lap and peered out the window at the barely visible outline of an enormous square building that seemed to take up the whole block. In the dark, it looked mysterious, filled with secrets.

"That's five times the size of my old school!" I said. "How many kids go there?"

"About a thousand at this one," Uncle Mack said. "Hampton's got four other junior highs. And four high schools."

"A thousand!?!" In a junior high, that'd make over three hundred kids in each grade! "Are you sure?" I asked Uncle Mack. "How can a thousand kids go to one school?"

"Don't you go getting cold feet now," he said. "Back home, you'd have been bused over to Tyler High this year. That's a pretty good sized place, too."

"That's true." I crumpled up the milk carton in my hands. "But this school's still a monster."

"Nothing to be scared about," Aunt Louise said as Uncle Mack pulled the pickup into the dirt driveway beside a long, narrow white house.

"In the South they call this a shotgun house, a house with all its rooms in a row," Uncle Mack said. "Ever see one back home?"

32

"Not with two front doors." I followed them across the small yard. "Why's it have two front doors?"

"A double-barrel gun, this one. It's called a duplex. A retired couple lives on the other side. Mr. and Mrs. Freeley. The Freeleys own the house; we rent from them." Uncle Mack unlocked one of the doors. "Not much of a place. Hope you weren't expecting something lavish."

"You'll have to sleep on the pull-out couch in the front room here," Aunt Louise said as we entered the house. "I think we best all get right to bed considering it's so late and you been on a bus hours on end. Tomorrow's a big day for you."

Alone on the sofa in the dark, I was wide awake. Aunt Louise thought a thousand kids was "nothing to be scared about." But I was used to a small school. Seventh and eighth grade are still in grade school at home and, since folks don't like to bus younger kids far, small schools are spread all over the county. In my eighth-grade class in Tyler, there were only forty-two kids. I knew all of them.

I turned over onto my side, trying to get comfortable in my new bed. My brain raced. This was the year for mustering up courage, I thought. Grade school was over, no matter where I lived. If I'd stayed in Kentucky, I'd be facing high school. Mustering up courage to face Tyler High would have been easier, though. At Tyler, I'd have forty-one definite friends!

Shifting from one position to another, I stayed awake most of the night. Before daylight, I heard Uncle Mack humming quietly in the kitchen. He was probably getting ready for work. Sometime after the pickup pulled out of the driveway, I finally fell asleep and woke up to the sound of eggs spitting grease in the kitchen. Aunt Louise fed me a big breakfast I didn't want, gave me money to buy lunch at school, and hovered over me at the front door.

"I've got you enrolled already," she said. "All you have to do is give them the papers from your school in Kentucky. You got them with you?"

"Yes, ma'am."

"You got plenty of time. You seen the school as we came in last night. It's only six blocks — no way you can get lost."

Nearing Hampton Junior High, I saw other kids hurrying toward the front entrance of the school. Three stories tall and stretching almost the whole length of the block, the building looked even larger than it had the night before. It seemed warm and friendly in daylight, though; the yellow bricks gleamed in the morning sunlight and I thought of the rust-streaked old gray cinder blocks of my grade school in Tyler.

As I crossed a brick walk to the front door, I glimpsed faces in the second-floor windows. The unknown faces scared me; I shivered and looked back down, staring at pictures and words scrawled onto the bricks, some chiseled into the pavement, some added in crayon or chalk, smudging fast under the shuffling feet of the first day of school. From some of the words and pictures, ugly thoughts leaped up at me.

I found the office and gave a secretary my papers from Kentucky. After she put things in order in my file, she handed me a schedule for my classes and rushed me out of the office, leading the way up a staircase jammed with students running up and down. On the second floor, I didn't have much time to look around, but I noticed wide, butter-colored lockers as high as my head on both sides of the long hall. Together with the bright lighting, they made it a pleasant, cheerful place compared to the gloomy halls in my grade school with their dim lighting and dull, dark green lockers.

As I followed the secretary, the noise of so many people

began to make my head ache. Boys talked loudly or shouted, some of them popping gum and reaching out to slam their fists on the lockers. Girls walked in bunches, glancing up quickly and lowering their voices to whispers and giggles as the boys passed. A few of the girls wore jeans and simple shirts or blouses like the short-sleeved turquoise blouse I had on with my own jeans; Mama bought me three cotton blouses in pastel colors at an end-of-the-summer sale in Tyler. Most of these girls, though, wore wool dresses or pleated skirts and wool sweaters. I thought they must be sweating on a hot day, just so they could show off their new fall clothes.

In front of me, the secretary pointed to a door on the right. "This is your homeroom," she said.

What was I supposed to do here? Back home, eighth-graders didn't have homerooms or change classes. We stayed in the same room all day.

"Good luck, honey," the secretary said, turning and disappearing down another staircase.

I stood alone outside the door, wishing I was still in Mrs. Swiggett's eighth-grade class. She taught us English each morning and then left to teach in lower grades while teachers for other subjects came to our room. At the end of the day, Mrs. Swiggett came back to our class. Everything was simple.

Swallowing to relieve the burning in my stomach and chest, I stepped from the hallway into my homeroom. I was afraid to look at the other students already seated in the rows of desks, so I looked up at the lights in the high ceiling. Could these kids see the pounding movements of my heart? Clutching my canvas-covered notebook to my chest, I focused my eyes on the places where the steel pedestals of the desks were bolted to the floor. As I walked toward the end of the first row, the aisle seemed to tilt under my feet. Finally, my heart pounding harder, I steadied myself and slipped into the last seat.

A woman entered the room and seated herself behind the large pine desk in front. I gazed up into a blur of gray: steel gray hair, silver-rimmed glasses, a grayish-blue cotton dress. Then my eyes met an intense frown on the face of a blond-haired girl in the seat next to me. Trying to ignore her, I stared down at the top of my desk and ran my hand across its smooth, cool surface. All the desks in Mrs. Swiggett's room had slanted, warped tops with words and initials carved into the old, dark wood.

A low, soothing voice began to call the roll and I pressed my hands down tightly on the desk top, bracing myself for the minute when I would have to speak.

"Mary Fred Pratley," the teacher read.

I raised my hand. "Here," I mumbled. "And, ma'am, I would like to be called Mary."

"Pardon?" asked the teacher.

I swallowed hard. "I would like to be called Mary," I said more loudly.

"All right," the teacher agreed instantly.

I watched the woman as her large wrinkled hand picked up a short pencil and made a line on the paper, crossing out the name Fred. Good.

The blond girl snickered and tapped the shoulder of a skinny boy in front of her. "Hey, Bobby! Did you catch that? A girl named Fred," she hissed.

Bobby laughed.

The teacher called the next name.

All morning I had to ask directions from each teacher to find my next class. After fourth period, I ate my lunch alone in the cafeteria and allowed myself time to go to the girls' bathroom before my fifth class. Inside the large bathroom I saw a row of small white sinks with metal-framed mirrors over them and, across from the sinks, the stalls with toilet bowls. As I went into an empty cubicle and locked the door, I heard the loud chatter of a large group of girls coming into the room.

"I got stuck with old-man Dolsey for English," a whiny voice complained. "He's so weird. He scares me. I'm serious. Besides, I wanted Mr. Paxton."

"Me, too. Oh, he's gorgeous!"

"Did you see him today? He's grown a mustache since last year."

"My twin sister's in his class. She gets all the luck."

"You've got a twin? I didn't know that!"

"Oh, gross!" the whiny voice said. "I spilled something on my sweater."

"You're such a slob, Roberta," someone teased. Several girls laughed.

When I came out of the cubicle, the girl named Roberta was pulling her sweater off over her head. She was the blond from my homeroom. She soaped up a paper towel and rubbed it over the soft pink wool of an expensive-looking sweater. Cindy Lou and I saw sweaters like hers in a store in Rollinsboro one time; they were real lamb's wool. I wondered if Roberta's lovely sweater had a stain. Maybe she just wanted an excuse to show the other girls she was wearing a bra and needed one more than any of them did, too.

At one of the sinks, I washed my hands in the orange water from the rusty tap. Roberta spotted me.

"Hey, everybody!" she said. "There's a new girl! She's in my homeroom. Her name's Fred! Isn't that a kill?"

Laughing, Roberta walked over and poked my shoulder.

"How're you doing, Ph-red?" She pulled the sweater back on and laughed again. "Let's get out of here," she said, and all the girls followed her.

I dried my hands on a paper towel. I wondered if all those girls liked Roberta. Maybe some of them would like to have a new friend. Nobody had given me mean or hateful looks except Roberta. And none of them had laughed at me with her. Still, I had a feeling Roberta was a ringleader. And not a single person had spoken to me the whole day.

I washed my eyes with cold water because I'd started crying just like a silly five-year-old. Then I ran a comb through my long hair and examined myself in the mirror. I liked my wavy red hair, but I wished I had shining blue eyes like Daddy's. Every last one of us girls got Mama's brown eyes; mine were almost black. Suddenly, I remembered how my father used to sing to me – or Mama or Cindy Lou, whoever was closest for him to grab: "Beautiful, beautiful brown eyes; I'll never love blue eyes again."

I smiled when I thought of Daddy's song and hummed it to myself all the way to English class. Roberta had big breasts for a ninth-grader, but her ugly whitish hair hung thin and straight and her eyes were a watered-down gray. She wasn't pretty; anybody in his right mind could see that.

Almost all the seats were filled when I got to English. I took a desk in the last row by the window and looked up at the blackboard. The board was clean except for the teacher's name in big chalk letters: MR. DOLSEY. That was the name I'd heard Roberta mention in the girls' room.

A minute after the bell rang, the teacher walked in and all the kids stopped talking. I looked up at a tall, heavy-set man wearing baggy black pants and a white, short-sleeved shirt,

38

clean as new snow. The button-down collar was open at his neck. I guessed he didn't know how to iron, though, and didn't live with anyone who did, because his nice shirt was wrinkled. He pulled a thin blue paper from the shirt pocket and began to call the roll, pacing back and forth across the front of the room while he read the names. Because he had a bad limp, his heavy black shoes clomped on the tile floor in a strange, spooky rhythm.

I planned to ask Mr. Dolsey to call me Mary when he got to my name — I did that in every class the first day — but I lost my nerve. I didn't think I could get his attention, anyway; as he called each name, his huge bug-out blue eyes glanced in the *direction* of the student who said "here," but he didn't really look *at* the person.

After he called the roll, Mr. Dolsey leaned up against his desk and ran one hand across the shiny bald top of his head. What little hair he had was blond but turning gray; it grew over his ears and around to the back of his neck. "This is primarily a writing course," he said, pinching his cheeks with his fingers and then pulling down his right ear lobe. "You will write a paper almost every week."

Mr. Dolsey spent the rest of the hour discussing the contents of our grammar book and describing the kinds of papers we'd write. He walked from one end of the room to the other, up and down the aisles, all the time he talked. He said we'd do no creative writing — no fiction or poems — but only exposition, writing that intends to explain or interpret. "The purpose of expository writing is to convey information clearly or to explain what is difficult to understand. It's a presentation or interpretation that embodies an analysis of the subject matter."

Some students around me whispered or grumbled in complaint, but I listened carefully. "We will emphasize two things,"

Mr. Dolsey said. "We will concentrate on content and clarity. You must be willing to think in order to develop and analyze ideas. And you must work hard on matters of grammatical correctness in order to communicate those ideas clearly."

Mr. Dolsey continually pulled on his ear lobe; it turned a dark purple color. "For tomorrow," he said from the back of the room, "you will read the material in your grammar book – Chapter 1, the first eight pages – on sentence fragments. Do the first five exercises. Then skip to Chapter 17, on paragraphing, read the first eight pages there, and write two paragraphs of expository prose."

The students groaned.

Mr. Dolsey returned to his desk and pinched his cheek with his fingers again. His eyes roamed the room, never settling on anyone; I couldn't figure out exactly where he *was* looking, but he seemed to roll his eyes in my direction quite often.

"The paragraphs don't have to be turned in tomorrow," Mr. Dolsey said. "They can be rough drafts, but you must have them for class discussion."

"He's the hardest teacher in the whole school," a girl behind me whispered to the boy beside her. Maybe so, I thought, but I felt excited. I was going to learn a lot about writing in this class. Roberta was right about one thing, though: Mr. Dolsey was weird.

Chapter 4

A BLOCK from home that afternoon, a girl came running up behind me.

"Hi!" she said. "You must live right on my street." She laughed. "I mean, since this is a dead end and you're on it, you must live here."

"Yes," I said.

"I'm Mattie Garrett." The girl slowed her walk to my pace. That took some effort because she had the longest legs I'd ever seen on a girl.

"I just moved in with my aunt and uncle," I said. "In the white house at the end."

"Oh, the Pratleys. That's just two houses down from me. On the other side of the street, though. What's your name?"

"Mary Pratley."

"I don't know them too well, but my father's friends with Mr. Pratley. I remember when they moved in. Last February. Valentine's Day. They're from Kentucky, aren't they? Are you from Kentucky, too?"

"Yes. Uncle Mack's my daddy's little brother."

Mattie turned around on the sidewalk, walking backward so that she faced me. She raised her voice. "You know what? I bet your uncle told Daddy you'd be moving here. Daddy didn't even tell me! He forgets everything interesting. That's obnoxious!" She turned back around, walking beside me again. "Daddy sees Mr. Pratley every day. They work together in the shipyard."

"Your daddy's a welder, too?"

"Yeah. And my grandfather. He's retiring next year, though. Daddy and Granddaddy and your uncle are all working on an aircraft carrier for the Navy now." Mattie shifted her books onto her other arm. "My father goes crabbing with your uncle, too."

"I've never even seen a crab."

"Kids at Hampton High, they call their football team the Crabbers. You stay around here and you'll see plenty of crabs. Daddy and Mr. Pratley met this guy named Lyndon Smith, a big boss over at the shipyard, and he lets them tie up crab pots to his pier." Mattie shifted her books again. She sure was a talker. "Mr. Smith lives right on Chesapeake Avenue. Has his own pier running out into Hampton Roads behind his house — almost like he owns the water."

"How do you put a pier on a road?"

Mattie smiled. "Hampton Roads is a big stretch of water that runs out to the Chesapeake Bay. People call this whole area Hampton Roads."

"Oh," I said. She probably thought I was really dumb. "I'd like to see a place like that Mr. Smith's."

"You'll see it. Daddy and your uncle go over there pretty often and check the pots to see what they got."

Mattie stopped in front of a little blue house on the right.

The paint was peeling off the front. "This is my place," she said. "Listen, why don't you come in and have a cold drink?"

We dropped our books on the front stoop and went inside. "Mama's not home," Mattie said, heading for the kitchen.

I waited in the living room. A picture of a huge ship hung over the sofa. Mattie saw me staring at it when she came back with the two cans of Coke.

"That's the USS *Enterprise*," she said. "Granddaddy talks about it all the time. He worked on it over twenty years ago; it's a famous aircraft carrier."

"Why?"

"What?"

"Why's it famous?"

"I don't know." Mattie grinned. "I don't always listen when he's talking."

"It's beautiful," I said.

"Granddaddy gave us the picture. He helped build the *United States*, too. That was a passenger ship. It set a speed record for going across the Atlantic."

"You must have listened when he talked about that one."

"Yeah. I've got a picture of it in my room; I'll show you sometime."

Mattie handed me one of the Cokes. "Let's go sit on the stoop. It's too hot in here."

We sat on the top step. Mattie's legs stretched over all three steps and out into the yard.

"So," she said, "what do you think of this place?"

"The neighborhood? Or the school?"

"Both."

I wished she hadn't asked me. I looked at the small frame houses crowded together on the block. Most of the porches had dirty black screens. Dying grass covered the tiny yards. I felt happy that Uncle Mack was out of the coal mines, but this place sure wasn't what I'd expected or hoped to find.

"I like the school," I said. "And I guess the neighborhood's not so bad." I didn't want to tell my disappointment to Mattie; after all, she lived here. But it seemed like people on this street worked and struggled nearly as hard as folks back home and didn't have much more to show for it. What's more, they had no forests or wild animals or broad open fields with dew on the grass. Maybe the ocean was nice, though. Maybe I'd like crabs and other sea creatures when I learned about them.

"You got the biggest house on the whole street," Mattie said.

"The house just looks big because it's made for two families. The inside's small. The whole house is like a hallway."

"What?"

"All the rooms are in a straight line," I explained. "You go into the front room, then straight into the kitchen, and straight on into the bathroom, and then straight into the bedroom."

"Well, you can't get lost in there."

"It's got windows only on one side except in the front room and bedroom. The whole place is dim like the hall at my old school. I sleep on a fold-out sofa in the front room."

"We've got two bedrooms, but I have to share with my brother. He's absolutely obnoxious. He's in eighth grade. What grade are you in?"

"Ninth."

"Me, too. I'm too old to be sharing with Norman. We have this tall partition right down the middle of the room, but there's not enough privacy. My parents can't afford a bigger house, though. I'm stuck with him." She wrinkled her nose in distaste at the thought of her brother and took a big swallow of her Coke. "Now," she said, "tell me everything you think about Hampton Junior High."

I told her what courses I had and about my teachers. Mattie talked and laughed so easily that I was thinking about telling her what had happened in homeroom and the bathroom with Roberta. Before I got a chance, though, a boy taller than Mattie came running up into the yard. Staring at his thick sandy hair and beautiful green eyes, I tried to hide my astonishment when Mattie introduced him to me as her brother. Norman was what Mama calls "drop dead good-looking." How could Mattie call someone like that "obnoxious"?

Norman didn't even say hello. He just stood there. I guess if you look like Norman, though, you don't have to worry whether girls will like you or not. They will.

"You better hustle," Mattie said to Norman. "It's four o'clock. Everybody's going to get late papers today. Not that that's anything new."

"You're such a nag, Mattie," Norman said, walking between us up the steps.

"Some people don't get theirs until six o'clock," Mattie said to him. "You're going to get fired."

Norman went inside.

Mattie turned back to me. "He's got his whole life organized around newspapers. He's on the paper staff at school. He works on that an hour every afternoon and then he races home and delivers the *Times-Herald*. He reads and writes all the time. Thinks he's going to be a newspaper reporter."

"I bet he has lots of girlfriends," I said in my most casual tone of voice.

"Nope. He's too shy. He thinks he's the world's greatest with words, but put him in front of any female and he freezes —

can't think of a single word to say. Like just now when I introduced you. At home or with his buddies, he talks all the time. He's obnoxious."

I guess Mattie liked that word. After we talked a few more minutes, I told her I had to go home. "Aunt Louise'll be wondering where I am."

"It was fun meeting you. I won't be seeing you walking home very often, though. I'm in band . . . play the saxophone. I go in early, too. You'll have to come over and visit me on weekends."

"O.K."

"I'll probably see you around school," Mattie said and went into her house.

Aunt Louise was frying chicken when I came in the back door. "How'd your day go?" she asked.

"Fine. Sorry I'm late. I stopped off at Mattie Garrett's."

"You met her?"

"Yes, ma'am."

"Isn't she a nice girl? Her daddy and brother go crabbing with Mack."

"She told me about Mr. Smith's house and their crab pots over there." I put my books on the kitchen table. "Can I help you get supper?"

"Sure can. We eat early. About four-thirty when Mack comes in from the yard. Hope that's O.K. with you."

"Yes, ma'am."

While we fixed supper, Uncle Mack came home in filthy clothes and headed straight for the shower. Then he got a can of beer from the refrigerator. "Come on out on the porch and tell me all about your new school," he said to me.

I hesitated. "I better help Aunt Louise."

46

"No, honey," said Aunt Louise. "All I have to do is mash the potatoes and we'll be ready to eat. Go on out there a few minutes and keep your uncle company."

On the screened-in porch, Uncle Mack asked about every single class and teacher I had.

"I read a lot," he said. "Didn't get to go to college, so I try to educate myself. Don't work at it hard enough, though." He sighed and smiled at me. "I play around too much, I reckon. If I'm not fishing, crabbing, playing baseball with men from the yard, or working on my pickup, I'm sitting here drinking beer. You like this porch?"

"Yes, it's nice." I guess Uncle Mack didn't notice the old porch sagging, the ugly gray tile loosening from the floor, or the thin plastic tearing away from the seats on the rusty glider. Or maybe those things didn't bother him.

"This is my favorite place," Uncle Mack said. "I sit out here every evening when I get home. I drink my cold beer, talk to your aunt Louise through that doorway, and listen to her chicken – or whatever's in the pan – frying. It's mighty fine in the fresh air."

"You two come on now!" Aunt Louise called.

After supper, Uncle Mack and Aunt Louise sat on the porch again, drinking coffee and talking. "Come on out!" Uncle Mack hollered to me. "Birds and crickets are singing." I stayed at the kitchen table, though. I had to read the first ten pages of my history book and the first chapter of my earth science book. I had to do those exercises on sentence fragments for Mr. Dolsey, too, and write two paragraphs of expository prose.

I sat at the table until Aunt Louise said it was time for bed. I wanted to get off to a good start, so I forced myself to concentrate on my homework and didn't think too much about my first day in the strange new school or about Roberta or Mattie or my new house. A couple of times, though, I found myself hoping I'd see Mattie's brother Norman at school the next day. And Mattie, too, of course.

Chapter 5

I SAW MORE places the first two weeks I spent with Aunt Louise and Uncle Mack than I'd seen my whole life altogether. On Labor Day weekend, we went one night to a drive-in movie that admitted a carload of people for a dollar and the next night to the amusement park at Buckroe Beach. We didn't ride many things at the park because of the money they cost, but Aunt Louise took me on a ride called a roller coaster and scared me to death. The next weekend, we spent all Saturday afternoon on the battlefield at Yorktown where General Cornwallis's troops surrendered to General Washington at the end of the Revolutionary War.

"Right where you're standing, freedom for our colonies began," Uncle Mack said.

"That was Seventeen Eighty-One," said Aunt Louise. "Over two hundred years ago."

Aunt Louise and Uncle Mack promised to take me to see Williamsburg, the colonial capital of Virginia. Aunt Louise said it was exactly like going back to the eighteenth century; all the buildings were restored and everyone who worked for what Aunt Louise called "the colonial restoration" wore eighteenth-century costumes.

I learned a lot from my aunt and uncle. The day after we went to Yorktown, Uncle Mack rented a tiny boat at a place on the James River called Red's Pier; he and I fished all day. We caught mostly rockfish.

"It's really a striped bass," Uncle Mack explained to me out on the river. "Lives part of the time in the ocean and comes up into the river's mouth to spawn."

"Does that mean reproduce?"

"Yep."

When we got home, Uncle Mack fried the fish in cornmeal. I ate four!

One Friday before supper, Uncle Mack came home, clomped his big rubber boots on the kitchen floor and pulled a can of beer from the refrigerator. "Sultry air out there for September," he said, popping open the can. "Clouds are ominous."

Aunt Louise set plates on the table and laughed. "Listen to those big words."

"Sure sign of an early frost."

"Mack," Aunt Louise said, "why don't you get out of that beer? You're getting fat again."

I glanced up from my books at the table and saw Uncle Mack pat Aunt Louise on the behind. "Man's got to have a little refreshment after a hard day," he said. "Ought to drink a beer or two yourself, Louise. Put some meat on those bones."

She shook her head and pointed to the green letters printed across her beige apron: THERE'S NO SUCH THING AS TOO RICH OR TOO SKINNY.

"That mean you're going to stop feeding me?" he asked.

"No, but I'm going to put you on a diet one of these days."

"Not tonight, I hope. Could you hold off supper, though? Let's go over to Smith's and check the crab pots before dark."

"All right."

Uncle Mack turned to me. "Want to go?"

"Sure! Mattie Garrett told me about that place. Can she go, too?"

"You bet. What're you doing slumped over those books on a Friday night, anyway?"

"Writing an English paper," I said, suddenly feeling depressed. "I've been working on it all week. It's due Monday."

"How's school going so far?" he asked.

"Terrible! I got *awful* grades on my first two English essays!" Surprised to hear myself shouting, I hit my knee with my fist. "I can't figure out what I did wrong!"

Uncle Mack put his hand on my shoulder. "Stay calm," he said. "What's your teacher say the problem is?"

"He hardly writes anything at all on the papers." I yanked the two essays from the back of my English notebook. "The first one was a description. I wrote about autumn in Kentucky." I read aloud the comment at the bottom of the last page. "Mr. Dolsey wrote, 'Grammar excellent. Content poor — you need more appeal to the senses and better use of detail.'"

When I tossed the paper down on the table, Uncle Mack picked it up, leaned up against the refrigerator, and began to read.

"He gave me a C on that!" I raised my voice. "I *never* got a C before! Not in anything! And English was my best subject back home." I flipped through the pages of the second paper. "He gave me a C on this one, too. It's a definition paper. I defined *friendship*."

"Is there a note on that one?" Aunt Louise asked.

"Yes. He says, 'Grammar excellent. Content too general — needs clearer illustration with specific, concrete details.'"

Aunt Louise sat down at the table and looked at me. "Is he right? Do you need to work harder?"

I shrugged. "I don't see why."

"How're your other classes going?" she asked.

"I'm doing good in math and science and history."

"Listen to this," Uncle Mack said, still leaning up against the refrigerator. He read from my first paper: " 'On the hills all over Dowell County, the leaf-covered trees turn bright and lovely colors. Motorists pull their cars to the sides of the road and sit to drink in the beauty.' "

"I think that sounds pretty good," I said.

"I probably couldn't have done better," Uncle Mack said. "Never claimed to be Shakespeare, that's for sure." He handed the paper back to me. "I like what he wrote about appealing to the senses, though. You know — adding details that make the reader see things, smell them, hear them. I like to read that kind of writing. You might have described the *exact* colors of the leaves, for example."

I didn't look at him as I put the two essays back into my notebook.

"Or the way light at different times of day changes the colors of the leaves," he continued. "Lord, it's a blazin' glory of —"

"Mack, for heaven's sake, slow down!" Aunt Louise said. "Mary Fred has to write the papers, not you."

"Just trying to help a little." He sat down and put his big hand on top of my notebook. "You better go talk with this Dolsey fellow. Let him tell you what the trouble is."

"I don't want to talk to him," I said.

"Why not? You don't like him?"

"I don't know." I drew in a deep breath and let it out slowly. "He explains things well and makes everybody work hard. I have to admit he's a good teacher. In class, anyway.

52

But those grades upset me! He should have written more comments on my essays; I don't think they're bad."

"Why don't you want to talk with him?" Aunt Louise asked.

"He's kind of creepy." I ducked my head, not sure whether I should go on. "In the bathroom at school, I heard a girl say that he scares her. She's not a nice girl and I don't like her so I didn't pay much attention, but after I got in his class, I started thinking about her saying that."

"Do you know why she's scared of him?" Uncle Mack asked. "Why'd you say he's creepy?"

"I can't explain it. But he makes me jittery. He paces all over the room — he can't stand still a minute. And he pinches his face and ears. He's just so strange — he's a bald old man about fifty years old —"

I stopped talking because Uncle Mack was laughing. "Isn't that something?" he said to Aunt Louise. "This child thinks fifty years makes an old man. That beats all."

"Isn't that pretty old?" I hesitated. "How old are you?"

"Thirty-six. Still a spring chicken. Louise there, she's a baby. Twenty-five."

"See? He's twice her age. He's old. And he's . . ."

"What?" Uncle Mack asked.

I traced my fingernail around the pattern of a butterfly on the Formica tabletop. "He's fat," I said and went on quickly, "and he stares at me without looking at me. All the time. For no reason."

Aunt Louise raised her eyebrows. "He stares at you without looking at you? What're you talking about, honey?"

"I don't know how to tell you. I guess you'd have to be around him to understand."

"Well, I think you better talk with him, anyway," Uncle Mack said. "But put up those books for now. We've got to get to the bay before dark. Run over and see if Mattie wants to go. Or call her."

"I'll run over," I said.

Mattie and I rode in the back of the truck with two washtubs. One of them had half-frozen herring in the bottom.

"That's bait," Mattie told me. "It'll be thawed by the time we get there. You put it in the crab pots before you throw them back in."

I wasn't prepared for the beauty of Chesapeake Avenue. Tall, elegant brick homes hid behind shrubs and huge old trees across the avenue from Hampton Roads. The same trees I always saw in Kentucky—evergreens, dogwoods, magnolias, and maples—stood taller and lovelier here, as if proud to shade the green lawns and line the brick driveways.

Uncle Mack drove onto a gravel road marked "Private" at the end of Chesapeake Avenue and pulled the pickup into a driveway several houses down.

"Isn't this something?" Mattie asked, gawking at the three-story brick house.

"It looks like one of those mansions I've seen in history books," I said as Uncle Mack came around to the back of the truck. "Like the plantation houses before the Civil War."

"Some of those are still standing along the James and York Rivers," Uncle Mack said. He helped us down from the truck. "You can go on tours through them."

"This one must have thirty rooms!" Mattie said. "Does Mr. Smith own the whole shipyard?"

"Probably just the submarines and the passenger liners," joked Uncle Mack.

"Yeah." Mattie nodded her head and pointed toward a large stone house farther down the road. "A girl who goes to our school lives there. I bet her father owns the aircraft carriers."

Uncle Mack took the tub with the herring in the bottom. "Grab the other one," he said to me.

I swung the washtub as we walked away from the house. We crossed a yard the size of a football field and started down a gentle slope toward the water.

"Can you believe this?" Mattie asked. "They've got enough land to put twenty houses from our street right on this lawn!" She looked back over her shoulder. "I sure would like to go in that house. Think I should go knock on the door and say I need a drink of water?"

I laughed and banged my tub up against her leg. "Why don't you just tell them to serve us a mint julep down at the pier?"

On the other side of the gravel road, we stood on the sandy beach. I drew in a deep breath of the salty-smelling air. I'd never seen any place so beautiful. The water was shallow close to the shore and under the pier; beyond that, Hampton Roads spread as far as I could see. The sun, going down behind us, threw its last light across the blue-gray water.

Aunt Louise took off her shoes. "Look here," she said. She stooped over to pick up a red bucket and a shovel, a kid's toys rusting in the wet sand.

Mattie and I followed Uncle Mack up onto the pier. He went right to work. Pulling on heavy rubber gloves, he began to yank the lines to the crab pots he had tied to the pier. Mattie and I stood close to him. I was surprised when I saw the edge of a pot coming up out of the water; it looked like a small cage made of thin wire mesh.

"That's a basket made from Mama's chicken wire," I said as Uncle Mack hauled the pot up onto the pier. I jumped back. The pot was over half full of live creatures, each one bigger than my fist. I barely got a good look at them before Uncle Mack slid open the top of the cage and stuffed his hands down into a tangle of crab legs.

"They're going to bite you!" I said.

"I imagine one or two of them'll do just that before I'm done." He tossed the crabs, one after another, into a washtub. In the tub, they crawled over one another on odd-looking legs, scrambling so fast I couldn't count the legs on a single one of them. When the pot was empty, Uncle Mack put some of the herring in the bottom part – "the downstairs half," he called it – and threw it back into the water; then he moved down the pier and pulled up another one.

"Those are blue crabs," Mattie said to me as Uncle Mack pitched more crabs into the washtub.

"They don't look blue." I leaned over to peer into the tub. "They're more like olive green."

"It's their top shell that looks that way. Daddy says that's a sure sign of a strong, healthy crab. They got traces of blue underneath, though. Pick one up and look."

"You're crazy!"

Mattie grinned. "Scaredy-cat!"

Two seagulls swooped down over our heads. Then they soared up again, calling to one another and racing across the water.

"That looks like fun," I said. "They're so graceful."

"Just like me." Mattie flung her arms up and down and twirled around in circles.

"Are you imitating a ballet dancer?"

"No, a seagull. Obviously you have no imagination."

Aunt Louise came up onto the pier.

"Feast your eyes," Uncle Mack said to her. "I got some real beautiful babies here."

"Mostly sooks," Aunt Louise said.

"What's a sook?" I asked.

"Sooks are mature females," said Mattie. "They've moulted their last time; once they've shed their last outside skeleton, they're grown ladies."

"How come most of them have red tips on their claws but some of them don't?"

"Bring that other tub down here," Uncle Mack said, heading for the far end of the pier.

Mattie picked up the washtub. "Just the sooks have those red claw tips. Crabbers say they know the lady blue crabs every time – they paint their fingernails bright red. Their boyfriends are called Jimmies. Jimmies don't paint their fingernails."

"Hey, you showoff," I said. "I'm impressed. You're way better at biology than dancing. You know all about this stuff, don't you?"

"I ought to. Daddy and Norman are really big on crabbing. I've been out in the boat with them, too."

"You've got a boat?"

"Oh, no. Daddy and your uncle borrow one of Mr. Smith's boats sometimes."

Mattie carried the washtub down to Uncle Mack. Aunt Louise and I followed her.

"Got seven more beauties in this one," Uncle Mack said, throwing three or four crabs into the tub. "Got a hole in my glove, too. They're going to grab a finger any second."

"Do you have to hurl them so hard?" Aunt Louise asked. "If anybody knocked your head up against a tub like that, you'd have a headache for a week."

"Gotta work fast. It's them or me."

While Aunt Louise and Uncle Mack checked the rest of the

pots, Mattie and I walked along the beach. I'd never heard anything so lovely as the sound of the water splashing lightly onto the sand.

"I like to imagine what's going on under there," Mattie said, sweeping her arm in the direction of the water. "It's a whole secret life—fish, crabs, oysters, shrimp. All of them scurrying around. Making a living. Just like people."

I smiled at her. "That's what I do when I'm walking through the woods back home. I imagine what all the animals are doing."

We walked for a while without talking.

"Wouldn't you like to live over here?" Mattie asked, looking up at the Smiths' house when we headed back toward the pier.

"Yes. This is the prettiest place I've ever seen."

When we got back to the pier, Uncle Mack and Aunt Louise were gone. We ran to catch up with them. They already had the washtubs loaded onto the truck. Mattie and I climbed on. I moved fast to the corner of the truck bed, as far away from the washtubs as I could get; the crabs were a jumbled mass, each one trying frantically to get out. Mattie laughed at me. Uncle Mack beamed at his crabs again and tapped gently on the side of each tub.

"Don't let any of these get away," he said.

We got back to the duplex after dark. Mattie went home and Uncle Mack put the washtubs on the porch. He drank beer and watched the crabs while Aunt Louise and I made grilled cheese sandwiches and salad. All during supper, we talked about crabs. Actually, they talked. I could only ask questions.

"How come you got almost all sooks?" I asked.

"Thousands—maybe millions—of sooks out there this time of year," Uncle Mack said. "In mating season, female crabs travel from the rivers and from out in the Chesapeake Bay toward the saltier waters here in Hampton Roads. The sooks that have mated are moving again now. They're leaving the shallow waters – like over by Smith's place at low tide – and heading for the mouth of the bay. Sleep there all winter and spawn in the spring."

"Fall's good crabbing time," Aunt Louise said. "All the crabs are migrating. Weather's getting colder, temperatures falling. Most of the Jimmies have already headed out for deep water where it's warmer."

"Do you go out into deep water on the boat with Norman and Mr. Garrett?" I asked Uncle Mack.

"Nope. We work the marshy, shallow areas. Going next weekend. We try to catch some of the crabs that haven't migrated yet." He poured about half a jar of dressing onto his salad. "Crabbing way out in the Chesapeake is a job for a skilled waterman, a real pro who makes his living from the water. Did you know that more crabs for human consumption are caught in this bay than in any body of water in the world?"

"What's consumption?"

"Something you can eat."

"Consume your sandwich instead of talking," Aunt Louise said. "We'll be up half the night."

"She's right," Uncle Mack said to me. "Sooks are good picking crabs. You got to steam them first, put them in a pressure cooker and then keep them in the refrigerator overnight."

"And sit picking them all the long day tomorrow," Aunt Louise said. "Wish we had more Jimmies. Jimmies are easier to pick. They've got more meat, too. And it's whiter."

"You got so many," I said. "Do you eat all the crabs you get?"

59

"He hauled in a lot this summer," Aunt Louise said. "Sold some to men down at the yard. We freeze most of the meat, though. We'll be feasting on crabmeat all through the winter."

"We don't freeze *most* of it, Louise," Uncle Mack said with a look of amusement on his face. "You eat more'n half the meat while you're pickin' it."

Aunt Louise gave me a sheepish grin. "Reckon I do," she said.

After supper, I wrote a letter to Cindy Lou and Mama. Then I went out on the porch and watched the crabs. The bright red claws of the sooks faded to a soft, rosy color in the dim light that fell through the kitchen doorway. Not more than two or three of the crabs were Jimmies.

I watched the strange creatures a long time. I wondered if they were scrambling over one another so frantically in the tubs because they were scared. They're like me, I thought. They're out of the world they know and into a strange one. But I hadn't lost my freedom forever. The sooks, though, would never have a chance to show their courage, to swim through the shallow waters to safety. They'd never reach the mouth of the bay or sleep through winter or reproduce in spring. They'd been torn from their goals through no fault of their own. It wasn't fair.

When I went inside, I told Aunt Louise I didn't feel well and went to bed early. I couldn't sleep, though. I thought about Mattie imagining the secret life under Hampton Roads, all those creatures scurrying around. She understood how I felt about the forest creatures back home; they had their own secret lives, too. I didn't blame Aunt Louise and Uncle Mack for crabbing; everyone here did that, just like they hunted in Kentucky. But I wasn't going to watch while the sooks went into a pressure cooker. They belonged in the sea.

Since I couldn't sleep, I turned back on the light by the sofa bed. I took out the little pocket dictionary Mr. Hadley had given me and looked up the words Uncle Mack had used earlier that night—"sultry" and "ominous." I wrote out the meaning for them on two of my white cards. Then I made out a card for each of the other words I'd learned that night: sooks, moult, migrate, consumption, and waterman.

Chapter 6

THE LAST Monday in September, my homeroom teacher, Mrs. Graham, announced that we had to elect someone to represent the homeroom on student council. She suggested that we talk among ourselves for two or three minutes and decide whom we'd like to nominate. I flipped the pages in my science book until I found the day's assignment. I'd already read it, so I just gazed at the page.

In the aisle beside me, Roberta turned around in her seat to talk to the girl behind her. "Do you want to run, Jeannie?" she asked.

"I don't know. I don't think so."

Glancing at Roberta and Jeannie, I saw Jeannie toss her long black hair back over her shoulder.

"Why not?" Roberta whined. "You'd be great."

"I just don't want to."

Roberta turned back. Voices all around me buzzed, but I didn't hear anyone discussing the election. Mrs. Graham called the class back to attention and talked about how much potential leadership there was in this homeroom.

Suddenly, Roberta whirled around in her seat and whispered loudly to Jeannie. "I have a great idea!" she said.

Mrs. Graham asked for nominations. Roberta raised her hand.

"Yes, Roberta?"

"Mrs. Graham, every year my homeroom elects a girl to student council. I think we should have a guy this year. I nominate Ph-red Pratley."

One after another a giggle or a snicker burst forth; in a few seconds the whole class was laughing. I clenched my fists in my lap and stared down at my science text. The rest of the period blurred. I vaguely remember that Mrs. Graham finally got order in the room and Jeannie Johnston was elected student council representative.

After school, I found a note from Aunt Louise on the kitchen table next to a package. "I walked to the store," the note said. "Home soon. Love, Aunt Louise." The package was addressed to me. It was wrapped in brown paper, a grocery bag, and tied with heavy string. Once I got it open, I found a small box taped shut and a letter on top of the box. The letter, written on school notebook paper, was from Cindy Lou.

Dear Mary Fred,

I might as well admit straight off as how I miss you. I think about you nearabout all the time, your letters coming often and things so different without you. I even miss fighting with you.

Mama's awful proud of your letters. Mr. Hadley come up to our place last night—yesterday was his 79th birthday!—and Mama read him ever last word of your letter what come the day before. Mr. Hadley brought coffee grounds for Mama. He had a little pouch of tobacco, too, and a package of cigarette papers. He rolled up cigarettes for himself while Mama read to him. He's fine-fingered — you know how he flicks his tongue over one of them papers and rolls up a cigarette with one hand, quick as you please.

Mr. Hadley said your writing was plumb fine. He run his hands over the pages of your letter just the way he does with his pine planks when he's making coffins. He said Mr. Dolsey must not know talent when he sees it. Then I made a big mistake — I said I didn't see why you call a C a bad grade. A C is a perfectly fine grade by me. Mama pointed her finger at me and told me how a C is fine only if it's your very best work. I wished I'd kept my mouth shut.

Mama's put out with my Cs. She thinks I can do better. I reckon I can. School's going good for me this year. And guess what? I'm in Mrs. Swiggett's room! No wonder you liked her so much. She's so nice! She's already helping me a lot, too. You were right that I need to improve my grammar.

After class today, Mrs. Swiggett asked me for your address. She said she's going to write to you soon. Lots of kids have asked about you, too. Everybody misses you, but I hope you've made new friends there. I bet you're already popular.

I got some good news. Folded in this letter is a newspaper article about Mama's wooden dolls! The fall art fair over in Tyler was last weekend. Mama sold all her dolls again — folks all over the place was talking about them. This reporter from over in Gatlinville, he took pictures of Mama's dolls and put them right in the paper! Mama's practically famous around here!

Well, I got to do homework now. It's a pain, especially without you here to help me. I hope you like the present from Molly and June. Write me soon.

Love,
Cindy Lou

I opened the newspaper article. There was a long story about mountain crafts and one of the pictures showed Mama's dolls.

64

In the caption under the picture I saw her name in bold type: BECKY PRATLEY. I smiled. Cindy Lou was right to be proud. Mama's wooden dolls *are* beautiful. Every night she's not sewing linings for Mr. Hadley or clothes for her kids, she's out in the kitchen carving. She can take a sprout of almost any kind of tree and as long as it has smooth bark and some little branches, she can whittle as pretty a doll as ever you'll see. She made one of those dolls for each of us girls and a wooden soldier for Daddy.

I pulled the tape off the box and opened it. Inside was a lady made of corn shucks with a red ribbon tied in the corn silk hair and with green ribbons tied tight around the middle of the husks to make a dainty belted waist. Molly had placed a letter in the box with the doll. Her letter was printed in all capitals. With lots of errors.

DEAR MARY FRED,
  IM IN SECAND GRADE NOW. JUNIES IN KENDERGARDEN. HERES A PRESENT FROM ME AND JUNIE. JUNIE INKED ON THE FACE BUT SHE DIDNT DO HER HANDS SO GOOD. SHE DOESNT GOT FINGERS. CINDY LOU DYES THE SKIRT. WITH DYE MAMA GOT FROM THE DENDRON LEAFS FOR YOU'RE COAT. I MISS YOU.

                    LOVE MOLLY ANN PRATLEY.

I smiled again. Molly meant rhododendron leaves. As I set the doll on a shelf over the kitchen table, Aunt Louise came in with two sacks of groceries. She noticed the doll right away.

"Molly and June made it," I said.

"Oh, let me see how they did that!" Aunt Louise picked up the doll gently. In the light in front of the window, she examined every detail, carrying on about the doll just like I knew she would. Aunt Louise is like Mama: she loves anything homemade. She sews and knits and crochets. She reads a lot, too, but if she doesn't have a book on her lap, she's got thread or yarn in one kind of needle or another, hurrying a mitten or a scarf or a sweater.

I got up and started putting away the groceries.

Reading my history assignment on the porch before supper, I heard voices arguing. I looked up and saw Norman on a bicycle in front of our house and Mattie in the yard carrying a stack of newspapers under her arm.

"You've got a lot of nerve!" Mattie hollered at her brother.

I went outside and walked up to them. "Hi," I said, forcing myself to keep my eyes on Mattie.

"Here's your paper," Mattie said, thrusting it into my hands but still glaring at Norman. "I can't believe his nerve," she said. "Asks me to help get the papers out and then comes wheeling up here fussing at me for not having this street done." She whacked Norman on the back with one of the papers. "This isn't *my* route!" she yelled.

Norman looked down at the yard and blushed. Really turned red. "I just said I wish you hadn't done this street last," he said. "I never leave my own street 'til last."

"Then do your own paper route!" Mattie said. "I'm never going to help you again."

Norman just stood there, one leg on the ground, one hanging over the side of the bicycle. The basket was filled with newspapers; the bike looked as if it was going to fall over.

Mattie turned to me and grinned. "Hi, yourself!" She set her stack of papers down on the ground beside her. "Hey, you don't look so good, Mary. You sick or something?"

"No."

"How come you haven't been over to see me?"

With the corner of one eye, I glanced at Norman. If he'd go

home, I could talk with Mattie. I didn't really want him to leave, though.

"I'm glad you're wearing jeans," Mattie said to me. "I wear jeans all the time. I only put on a skirt for church. Mama says I wouldn't look so tall if I wore skirts, but I hate them."

"You wouldn't look good in anything," Norman said, and grinned down at the yard.

I couldn't believe Norman was talking so much. I admit he wasn't exactly talking to *me*, but he'd said three whole sentences in front of me. He wasn't frozen the way Mattie said he is every time there's a girl around.

"Well," Mattie said suddenly, "you sure look down in the dumps, Mary. What's bugging you?" She put her hand on my arm.

"Oh, nothing much. There's this girl named Roberta Thompson and . . ." I stopped. I shouldn't have even said her name; I didn't want to talk about her in front of Norman.

"Oh, I know her!" Mattie said. "She's a mean one. She been hassling you?"

"Sort of."

"You know what? She lives over there on Hampton Roads in one of those houses down from Mr. Smith's. Remember the stone house I pointed to when I was talking to your uncle about those places? The one I said a girl from our school lives in?"

I nodded.

"That's her house! I'd have said her name, but I didn't know you knew her. She's spoiled rotten. Her father gives her everything she asks for."

"You're just jealous," Norman said, jabbing Mattie's arm lightly.

Mattie shoved him and the bicycle lurched. Norman leaped clear of it just in time to avoid falling, but newspapers flew all over the lawn when the bike toppled over. I figured Norman would be furious, but he just set the bike up with the kickstand and started picking up the papers.

"Nothing wrong with stating a true fact," he said. "You're jealous, Mattie."

"Shut up, Norman. You're so obnoxious. And you're never going to be a writer. Anybody who says 'a true fact' is never going to be a writer. Every fact is true by its very nature, so you don't say 'a true fact.' How redundant! And I'm not jealous of Roberta Thompson, so shut up!"

"That's redundant," Norman said. "You already said that once." He winked at me. I swear! I couldn't believe it! Maybe Mattie was wrong about him being so shy. Of course, the wink was to poke fun at Mattie, not to flirt. But it *was* a way of talking to me.

Encouraged, I wanted to say something to him. I glanced around. Mattie was busy picking up some of the scattered newspapers. I picked up two and handed them to Norman.

"Thank you," he said.

"Your sister told me you want to be a reporter," I said quickly, watching Mattie's movements while I spoke. "You write for the school paper?"

"Yeah. A regular column."

"That's great!" I said, helping him gather up more papers. "I like to write, too. English is my favorite subject. I hope I'll see your column."

"It'll be out soon," he said, just as Mattie came over and plopped a big stack of papers into the bicycle's basket. I put mine on top of hers.

"It's getting dark," Norman said to Mattie. "I'll finish this street."

68

"Well, that's generous of you, especially since it's your job in the first place."

"See you later," Norman said to me. Oh, I'm not sure he said it *just* to me, but he had his face turned in my direction.

I wiped my sweaty palms on my jeans. I'd actually had a real conversation with Norman!

"Good riddance," Mattie said as Norman rode off.

Aunt Louise stuck her head out the front door. "Come in for supper, Mary Fred!"

"In just a minute!" I yelled.

"What's Roberta been doing to you?" Mattie asked.

I told her about Roberta hissing my name the first day of homeroom and how she took off her sweater in the bathroom later that day and teased me in front of the other girls. "This morning, she nominated a 'guy' named Ph-red Pratley for student council from our homeroom. I don't understand why she has it in for me."

"You shouldn't take any of that personally," Mattie said. "Roberta treats most people pretty mean. She thinks she's so special 'cause she's got blond hair and all those fancy clothes. She never wears the same thing twice, I swear."

"That sweater she had on's the prettiest one I ever saw."

"The one she was scrubbing in the bathroom?"

"Yeah."

"Well, I like yours."

"My sister Cindy Lou gave it to me right before I left; it's her only good one, but she made me bring it."

"Mary Fred!" Aunt Louise called.

"Coming!" I turned back to Mattie. "Why's Roberta so mean?"

"I don't know. That's just the way she is. Sometimes I feel sorry for her. Her mother ran off with some younger guy. Everybody in town knew about it. It's a shame, but Roberta doesn't have to be such a snot. She told one of my girlfriends that her daddy's buying her a brand-new sports car for her sixteenth birthday."

"She's nearly sixteen?"

"Yeah. She failed a grade. The year her mother ran off." Mattie picked up her newspapers and winked at me. "I see your aunt calls you the same name Roberta does," she said.

"Yeah."

"Listen, I think it's a really cute name."

"I don't. But I'm stuck with it."

"We all have crosses to bear. Mine's Norman."

I should be so lucky, I thought.

"See you!" Mattie shouted as she ran across the street.

Chapter 7

On Tuesday, the day after Roberta tried to get Ph-red Pratley elected to student council, I turned in my third theme in English. It was six pages long and I'd worked on it two hours every night for a week and almost all of the weekend before it was due. Our first two papers were assigned subjects, but Mr. Dolsey said this one could be on anything we chose. I was interested in what Mattie told me about the ships her grandfather helped build, so I went to the public library and got several books on the history of ships. The book I liked most was about aircraft carriers.

I began my work by narrowing down my topic. Mr. Dolsey was just like Mrs. Swiggett about that: you have to focus your paper so that it includes a lot of precise information about one subject; the reader doesn't learn much if you ramble all around making vague remarks about a million different things. I think I might have been a little too general in my first two papers; Uncle Mack seemed to agree with Mr. Dolsey's notes about that when he read aloud the example from my description paper.

In class, Mr. Dolsey had been giving us examples of the difference between broad, general comments and exact, specific ones. He gave us homework exercises to work on this problem, too. What he said made sense, so I narrowed my topic to the USS *Enterprise* and made notes full of detailed facts from what I'd read. Since the *Enterprise* was built at the Newport News Shipbuilding and Drydock Company where Uncle Mack worked, I asked him questions about it, too.

"I can't help you much," he said. "That ship was commissioned in Nineteen Sixty-One. I was thirteen or fourteen — your age. Back in Kentucky, I hadn't even heard of an aircraft carrier. I've read some about it, though. When it was built, it could operate about a hundred aircraft."

I put my notes in order and wrote the paper. I described the ship and the process of building it. I told how the USS *Enterprise* was unique because it was the first nuclear-powered aircraft carrier. The *Enterprise* had eight nuclear reactors and was over one thousand feet long.

I gave Uncle Mack the paper to read when I finished. He said it was good and that he learned a lot from reading it. There's one thing about writing, though: you usually can't trust the judgment of people who love you. They don't want to hurt your feelings; they'll act like you're Ernest Hemingway or Katherine Anne Porter nearly every time. But I trusted Uncle Mack's opinion.

Anyway, I guess I'm biased about my own writing, too, but I thought I'd done a good job, so when I got the paper back on Friday that week, the C+ at the bottom of the last page stunned me. My third C in Mr. Dolsey's class! He'd written no comments on the paper. At the end of the hour, though, he called me up to his desk and said we should discuss my essays, especially this third one, after school.

I felt tense the rest of the day. I couldn't imagine what Mr. Dolsey would say about that essay. Suppose I didn't agree with his comments? I'd be scared to argue with a teacher. And I couldn't ask him to change his mind and give me a better grade; that would be humiliating. Hadn't I added detail just like he'd said to do, though? I knew it wasn't just an average paper! Did I have to go on getting a C on every theme? I hadn't come all the way from Kentucky to collect a line of Cs on my report card.

By the end of the day I'd calmed down a little. I dreaded talking with Mr. Dolsey, but I didn't have any choice. I had to listen to whatever he said. And I had to be polite. When the last period ended, I walked to my locker, got all my books, and went to his classroom. He'd brought in another straight-backed chair and placed it beside his desk for me. While I seated myself, he closed the door.

"I appreciate your offer to talk about my papers," I said.

Mr. Dolsey stood by the windows. He had on baggy pants like always, dark blue ones this time, and a long-sleeved white shirt with the sleeves rolled up to his elbows and the collar buttons open. The collar was starched and the shirt pressed with nice creases in the sleeves. I'd never seen Mr. Dolsey in a shirt that wasn't wrinkled; I wondered why I hadn't noticed this one earlier in the day.

I pulled my essays out of the back of a notebook and set my books on the floor beside my chair.

"You look lovely today, Mary," Mr. Dolsey said from over by the windows. I doubted that he'd sit down; he's always moving around. Still, he'd put an extra chair at the desk.

"Thank you." I was wearing a gray pleated skirt and a long-sleeved blue blouse that Aunt Louise and Uncle Mack had bought me.

Placing my themes on the desk, I wondered how Mr. Dolsey would be able to see them even if he did sit there. The blinds

73

on the windows were closed almost all the way. The class-room was dim.

He walked back and forth for a minute. Then he began to ask me all kinds of questions about myself.

"You're new here, aren't you, Mary?"

"Yes, sir. I'm from Kentucky."

He smiled in my direction. "That's rather obvious from your accent. Why'd your family move to Virginia?"

"They didn't. I came here to live with my aunt and uncle."

"I see," he said.

What did he mean by that? Facing me, he pinched his cheek the way he does in class all the time. His huge blue eyes seemed to be staring at my blouse, but, as usual, I couldn't tell exactly where his eyes were focused.

"Mr. Dolsey," I said, "I'd like to improve in your class. I'm willing to work very hard. But I've . . . been disappointed with my grades."

"Why'd you do that?" he asked, still torturing his cheek.

I felt confused. "I didn't intend to turn in average-quality work. I thought I'd —"

"No, no. Why'd you have to leave home?"

What was he talking about? "I thought the schools here would be better," I said. "I want a good education so —"

"Were you in trouble?"

I studied the pattern on my skirt. Surprising me, Mr. Dolsey came over and sat down at his desk. He didn't even glance at my papers, though.

"You weren't in trouble, Mary?" he asked.

Suddenly I realized what kind of trouble he might be talking about— *that* kind of trouble. Did I *have* to answer these embarrassing questions? I twisted a strand of my hair. Why would someone like Mr. Dolsey try to make me feel embarrassed? He was a teacher. Maybe he didn't realize the questions upset me.

"No, sir," I said. "I wasn't in trouble. I wanted to go to school here. My family can't afford four years for me at a university, so I want to do well in good schools and try to win a scholarship. I'll get a job, too, to help pay my expenses."

He didn't look at me while I answered his question; he still seemed to be staring at my blouse.

"Do you miss your boyfriend?" he asked.

That *was* what he was talking about! I twisted a piece of my hair again. "I don't *have* a boyfriend," I said. I took a deep breath and swallowed hard. "Mr. Dolsey, I'd like to talk about my papers."

"Why are you pulling your hair like that, Mary? You'll mess it up. You have such beautiful hair." Suddenly, he leaned closer to me and ran his fingers down the back of my head.

Still breathing deeply, I quickly slid my chair a little way back from his desk, pulling my head out from under his hand. What was wrong with him? I wanted to leave. How could I leave, though? He hadn't said one single word about my work. Wasn't I going to find out anything about my grades? Tears began to smart in my eyes; I widened them so the tears wouldn't spill. Maybe he didn't care about my writing at all. Maybe he wasn't the least bit interested in it. Why'd he write those notes on my first two papers, then? Just because that was his job and he was supposed to write comments? And why'd he ask me to come talk with him today?

I tried to keep my voice steady. "Please tell me what's wrong with my themes," I said.

He picked up my papers. "You said you'd like to go to college," he said. "What do you plan to study?"

"I want to be an English teacher."

Right away Mr. Dolsey smiled and made a funny little grunting noise. I realized he was amused. He didn't think I could do it. The tears stinging my eyes began to spill onto my cheeks. I tilted my head forward so my hair would fall around my face and eyes.

"I did well in English in Kentucky," I said, forcing the tears back. "My teachers there encouraged me. I don't understand why you think my writing's poor."

"Did you consider carefully the criticisms on these themes?" he asked, stacking the essays neatly on his desk. "You're going to need my help if you want to do better in this class." He gazed at the top page of the first essay on the pile. "Consider the manner in which this theme begins." He pointed a finger a few lines down.

Since I couldn't see what was written there, I leaned forward. When I did, Mr. Dolsey put his hand on one of my breasts.

I shoved back my chair and stood up, my heart racing.

"We can work together, Mary," he said.

As I bent down to pick up my books from the floor, he moved forward in his chair and placed his hand on my skirt, rubbing it across my behind. I jumped back from him and slammed up against a round metal wastebasket. It crashed over onto the tile floor, clanging loudly as it rolled back and forth. Shoving my books under one arm, I snatched my papers off Mr. Dolsey's desk, ran from the room, and went out the rear door of the school.

Outside, it had begun to rain. I raced across the west yard. My vision blurred by rain and tears, I almost slammed into a six-foot-high chain link fence that separated the yard from Sixth Street behind the school. I'd headed the wrong way. Trying to calm myself, I looked at the fence. Wind and rain had pounded links loose from the ground just the way they

76

did the chicken wire on our place back home. I stared at candy and chewing gum wrappers, napkins, and brown lunch bags trapped in holes in the fence. The letters on the candy wrappers jumped up and down. Turning away from the fence, I recrossed the yard. I walked rapidly past the ground-floor windows of the school and made my way to the street.

On the sidewalk, I gripped my books and essays tightly with one hand and wiped my eyes with the back of the other. Anger and shame forced tears from my eyes in streams. Why'd Mr. Dolsey think he could do that to me? Why had he chosen *me*? I thought of his comment about my accent and his amusement at the idea of me becoming a teacher. Did he think I was dumb? That I wouldn't even catch on to what he was doing? Maybe he thought I wouldn't care. All those creepy questions he'd asked me — was he making up his mind that I was a bad girl who'd been in trouble? Did I seem like someone cheap?

I quit fighting the tears and gave in to sobs, furious with myself. I'd taken so *long* to figure out what he was getting at with those questions! I never expected . . . I wiped my eyes again. He was a teacher! Like Mrs. Swiggett! I wasn't sure at first what he meant. And I was so worried about my stupid grades and then I started getting all teary-eyed, right in front of him, because he hurt my feelings by not showing any interest in my writing. I *was* dumb! Even after I understood those ugly things he implied about me, I stayed longer because I just had to find out how to get an A in his class! Well, my grades in his class *were* important! I couldn't pretend I didn't care about them. And now I couldn't even talk to him about my papers.

Walking more slowly, I drew in big breaths of air, trying not to think about what I should have done in Mr. Dolsey's classroom. It was too late now. Still, I felt ashamed for not telling him off when he started hinting around about dirty things. Even then, though, I hadn't had the slightest idea he'd do what he did! I shivered in the cold rain. I wished I'd clobbered him, too, instead of running out of there like a coward. That was dumb, too. I let him see how scared I was of him. Well, I *was* scared.

A burning discomfort flared in my stomach. Scared. A coward. I stopped abruptly in the middle of the sidewalk. Roberta was afraid of Mr. Dolsey, too! "He scares me," she'd said. I tightened my fingers around my books. Could I ask her about that? The idea of trying to talk with Roberta made my stomach burn worse. I started walking again. "Forget it," I muttered to myself. I'd just have to stay away from Mr. Dolsey. I'd never let myself be alone with him again. But what was I going to do on Monday? I had to go back into that class and face him.

In front of Mattie's house, I wiped my eyes one last time and tried to pull myself together before I got home. I sure could use somebody to talk with. Mattie was probably still at band practice, though. And I couldn't tell Aunt Louise and Uncle Mack about Mr. Dolsey. They'd write Mama and she'd worry herself sick. They might even go over to the school and make trouble. Of course Mr. Dolsey would deny it all. He'd be really mad, too. I might fail his class.

I crossed the street. I had to think of something.

Mrs. Swiggett's letter came that afternoon. She didn't intend for me to get it on the worst possible day; life's just full of hateful little coincidences like that.

Dear Mary Fred,
I hope your life is flourishing. I want you to know how proud I am of you and how much I believe in you.

It's a delight to have your sister in my class this year. Cindy Lou has a bright mind and I believe she's developing motivation and self-discipline. Perhaps someday she'll do as well as you have done, though certainly I've never compared her work to yours. You're two individuals and each must perform at her own level of ability and strive for her own goals.

It was my pleasure to meet your mother at the art fair in Tyler. Cindy Lou introduced us. I'd never met either of your parents before, though my brother worked for years with your father in the mines and regarded both your parents with admiration and respect.

Your mother's crafts are truly works of art; she's a skilled and talented woman. Now that I've met her and learned more about her from others (including a marvelous newspaper article!), I'm even more convinced that you've been blessed with a wonderful family, Mary Fred. Your mother's faced tragedy with strength and dignity — and with more courage than perhaps you can yet understand. I hope that as you pursue your dreams, you'll always find a way to let Becky Pratley know you value her character and worth.

I trust you're pleased with your decision to go to Virginia and that you've found many of the benefits you sought. Please write and tell me how you are. I miss you, Mary Fred, and wish you all good things. I'll always believe in your enormous potential. You're a most promising English student; if you're willing to work very hard, I know that someday you'll be the very finest teacher.

Affectionately,
Norma Swiggett

Mrs. Swiggett's letter upset me. Why did she write so much about Mama? Was she criticizing me? Did she think I didn't respect my mother? Perhaps she just wrote all that because she was so impressed with Mama and wanted to give me some advice on being an appreciative daughter; Mrs. Swiggett's the "motherly" type. Even so, her words stung me.

I took the letter out on the porch and sat in the glider. Realizing it was Mama I wanted to talk with, I began to cry again. For a few minutes, I felt more homesick than I had in the whole month I'd been in Hampton. On the first day of school, I'd missed Mrs. Swiggett's class. Now I missed everything: the Kentucky hills and forests, my old friends, my sisters, and most of all, Mama. But my mother wasn't here and, since she couldn't help me from Kentucky, I didn't want to worry her. I had to figure out what to do on my own. Crying wasn't going to help, but I couldn't think of a single thing that would. I felt as helpless as the sooks Uncle Mack pulled up out of the bay.

I looked at Mrs. Swiggett's letter again. What upset me most about it was her praise of my "enormous potential" to become "the very finest teacher." If only she knew about Mr. Dolsey! At Hampton Junior High School, Mary Fred Pratley wasn't exactly "a most promising English student."

Chapter 8

MONDAY MORNING I was going through the English themes again when Aunt Louise and I got into a quarrel in the kitchen. I'd hardly slept the whole weekend and my stomach stayed twisted in knots. Sunday night I thought of saying I was sick, which was practically the truth, anyway, and staying home the next day. I couldn't do that forever, though. By Monday morning I knew I had to go to school; there was no way out of it. But how was I going to control my anger when I saw Mr. Dolsey again? One thing was certain: no matter how mad I felt, I had to keep my mouth shut around him until I figured out what was best to do about the problem.

"Didn't you talk with your teacher one day last week about your papers?" Aunt Louise asked. She had toast in the oven and was frying eggs.

"Yes."

"I meant to ask you about that. What'd he say?"

I didn't answer. I flipped through the essays again. I'd read the paper on the *Enterprise* a hundred times over the weekend; I searched for errors (I didn't find any), wondered whether the writing could have been improved, and tried to decide what to do about my grades.

"Mary Fred? What'd he say?"

I looked up, startled by Aunt Louise's voice. "Nothing very definite," I said. There was one more thing for me to worry about, I thought. Was it right for me not to tell Aunt Louise and Uncle Mack what was going on? Wouldn't they want to know? Could they help me?

Aunt Louise set milk and orange juice in front of me. "Better talk to him again, then," she said.

"I don't want any breakfast." I chewed on the corner of a fingernail.

"Honey, you can't go to school without something in your stomach. Why, breakfast is the most important meal of the day. I bet your mama's told you that." With a rubber spatula, she scooped the two eggs from the pan onto a plate. "You pick over your food every morning."

I bit the nail off and chewed it. "I'm not hungry."

"Dig in now." Aunt Louise set the plate on the table. "You're going to eat your breakfast, so let's not quarrel."

I stared at the greasy eggs. Silence closed over the kitchen. I drank some orange juice and kept my head down.

"I packed you a lunch," Aunt Louise said, surprising me. "There's cold chicken left over from last night's supper and biscuits and one of them apples Mrs. Freeley next door gave us."

I wanted to say "*those* apples, Aunt Louise," but instead I said, "I don't want to take a bag lunch. Uncle Mack gives me money to buy hot lunch in the cafeteria."

"I know that. But Mack and I have discussed it and . . ." Aunt Louise poured herself a cup of coffee and sat down with me. She tapped her long fingernails on the table. "Tell me why you don't want to take your lunch," she said quietly.

I pushed an egg around on the plate with my fork. "I don't

want cold chicken and hard biscuits and ugly little wormy apples like the Freeleys have."

"Why, Mary Fred, I'm put out with you today!" She walked over to the sink and stood with her back to me as if she were looking out the window. "What am I supposed to do with the nice lunch I've made for you?" she asked.

"I don't know." Why'd she have to get on me *this* morning? My head didn't have room for any more problems.

"I bet lots of kids take their lunches," she said.

"I don't want to eat food like that in front of the kids in this school!" I tried to stop myself, but the hateful words flew out of my mouth as if they were separate from me, not my doing. "That's what I always had to eat in Kentucky," I said. "I hate that stupid country food!"

Aunt Louise sucked in her breath. "If you were my child," she said, turning around, "I'd slap your face. I won't have you back-talking me like that. Do you understand?"

I kept my eyes on the eggs, still poking at them, but I nodded.

Suddenly, Aunt Louise sat back down. She sighed. "We're both in foul moods this morning, aren't we?"

I didn't say anything.

"I've been up sick all night." She gazed down into her coffee. "Mary Fred, some things are going to be happening with me and Mack. We don't have much money and we're saving to buy a house. We have to be more careful about what we spend." She took a swallow of the coffee and looked at me. "We just can't have you buy lunch every day."

I stayed quiet.

"In the years we've been married, I've cost us a pile. I've lost two babies from miscarriages. You know what those are, don't you?"

"Yes," I said. Mama told me about sex and pregnancy and childbirth when I was eleven.

"I spent several days in the hospital the last time it happened. That was right after your daddy died and Mack quit the mines. He was taking courses in welding and we didn't have medical coverage. My hospital stay put us awful in debt."

"I'm sorry. I didn't know any of that." Feeling a little ashamed for being such a brat, I ate a couple bites of an egg.

"We're doing a sight better these days, but we have to pay off our debts and save some. School lunches are getting expensive."

I finished my orange juice and looked up at the clock over the stove. "I better get going."

"O.K. It's turned pretty snappy out there. Your mama mentioned in her last letter that she'd woven you a new coat."

I pushed my chair back and grabbed my books. "Here comes more trouble," I thought. This day was sure getting off to a lousy start.

"Becky said she looked through several issues of *Seventeen* to get an idea for something fashionable but still plenty warm," Aunt Louise said. "Haven't you unpacked the coat? I'm anxious to see it and I think you're going to need it."

I walked over to the counter, picked up the lunch she'd packed, and stacked it on top of my books. Gripping the books fiercely, I eased toward the doorway to the front room. "I don't need a coat yet," I said.

"Goodness, do we have to argue about everything this morning? It's the first of October, honey; Indian summer's over. Where'd you put the coat?"

"Aunt Louise, I have to go. I'm going to be late."

She turned her coffee cup around and around in her hands. "You're acting awful peculiar. What's going on?"

84

"I don't want to wear the coat. I don't like it." I walked into the living room toward the front door.

Aunt Louise came right behind me. "Does your mama know that? Why don't you like it?"

"It's ugly," I blurted out. "It's got horrid loud-colored stripes — I'd stick out like a sore thumb if I wore it to school. I look about ten feet tall in it, too. And the sleeves are too big. The whole thing's too big — it's so full it makes me look like an elephant."

"Aren't you exaggerating? I can't imagine Becky making one of her younguns anything that far off in fit."

"Aunt Louise, these city kids don't wear homemade clothes!"

She looked right into my eyes. "You're mighty uppity this morning," she said softly. "Who do you think you are?"

"I could be pretty if I had some good dresses, a proper coat, and nice shoes — things like the skirt and blouse you and Uncle Mack bought me."

"You're already pretty. Maybe you need more clothes, but there's nothing wrong with the ones you do have."

"Nobody in this school would be caught dead in that coat! It looks . . . It looks tacky."

"Is that so?" Aunt Louise never took her eyes from my face. "I'll not ask you to look tacky, then. Don't even bother to unpack the coat. But you've got a few things to learn, Mary Fred. You're not what you wear. You are what you think you are."

I grabbed the door handle and ran out.

"You go right ahead and freeze!" Aunt Louise yelled after me. "For the whole winter, if you want to!"

I knew she was standing on the cold concrete stoop in her

bare feet. I didn't look back. I wasn't going to think about her. I wasn't.

I didn't see any kids at all on the street. All of Aunt Louise's questions and her preaching had made me late. I'd have to go to the principal's office and get a note to be admitted to homeroom. I'd walk in after it had already begun and that would be one more thing for Roberta to snicker about. Well, I had more important trouble to think about than Roberta. Or Aunt Louise.

I ran most of the way to school. Inside the building, I was almost to the office when I saw Norman at the other end of the hall standing beside a girl. They were talking. Norman was going to be late to his homeroom, too. It wasn't any business of mine, though. And why should I care if he was talking with some girl?

I wondered if the girl was pretty, but they were so far away that I couldn't tell. Instead of going straight to get my late pass for homeroom, I went to the girls' bathroom; I walked right past Norman and the girl. She wore glasses and had a long brown ponytail hanging down her back.

"Hi," Norman said.

Big deal. One word. I nodded at him but kept my eyes down. I'd been thinking he liked me because he'd said three or four sentences in front of me while he argued with his sister. How stupid can you get? He was having a whole conversation with that girl, a much longer conversation than the few words he'd said to me in the yard.

Pushing open the rest room door, I wished I had a friend to talk to about Norman, somebody who might know if that girl in the hall was his girlfriend. But I couldn't let Mattie know I liked her "obnoxious" brother. She might tell him.

86

Besides, I didn't know whether Mattie knew all that much about Norman and girls, anyway. She'd been *wrong* about Norman being shy. He talked to girls, all right. Just not in front of Mattie.

I went to the nearest sink and turned on the faucet. Washing tears from my face with cold water seemed to be a habit of mine.

I spent most of the morning turning myself into a worse wreck than I'd been all weekend. I wondered what would happen in Mr. Dolsey's class — what he would do around me, what I'd do around him, what he'd say, whether he'd be nervous. The class astonished me: everything went right on as if absolutely nothing had happened.

"Open your grammar texts to Chapter Six, the section on dangling modifiers," Mr. Dolsey said, heading for the back of the room with his typical restlessness. He began immediately to call on students to read sentences aloud and correct them.

Beside me, a girl named Patricia got a tube of lipstick and a compact with a mirror from her purse. As she smeared a deep purple color across her top lip, Mr. Dolsey returned to the front of the class. Patricia eased the compact and the open lipstick down by her side while a boy across the room struggled with the sentence Mr. Dolsey had asked him to correct: ". . . because the modifier doesn't refer to the right word," the boy was saying.

"How would you correct the sentence, then?" Mr. Dolsey asked, moving in the boy's direction.

I opened my book and tried to follow the exercises but I couldn't concentrate. My eyes wandered to the low shelf that ran the length of the room under the blackboard. Mr. Dolsey displayed all kinds of books and magazines on the shelf, propping them up to face the class. He borrowed books from the library and set them out, hoping to entice the nonreaders, I supposed. The magazines belonged to him; he allowed students to take them home overnight. Once I borrowed an *Atlantic Monthly* and read a short story in it.

I glanced over at Patricia just as she propped her compact on her book and edged the lipstick up to her mouth. She'd painted about half her bottom lip when Mr. Dolsey arrived right in front of her.

"Read the next sentence, Patricia," he said.

Patricia snapped the compact closed and jerked the lipstick back down beside her. "Although only ten years old," she read slowly, "my father expected me to work in the fields as hard as he did."

"What's wrong with that?" Mr. Dolsey asked.

Patricia gawked at the book and lowered her head. "I guess a ten-year-old . . . A ten-year-old couldn't work as hard as –" She stopped as the class began to laugh.

With an irritated gesture of his hand, Mr. Dolsey flicked away Patricia's answer. "Mary?" he said. "What's wrong with this sentence?"

He was calling on me just like always! I stared down at my book, the letters on the page fuzzy and blurred. With Mr. Dolsey's attention focused on me, I felt shame. I saw red blotches breaking out across the skin on my arms; I bet they were spreading just as red across my face. *He* was the one who should feel ashamed.

"Mary? What's wrong with this sentence?" Mr. Dolsey asked again. I bit down on my bottom lip. He had no right to do what he'd done and then act as if nothing had changed!

"Mary?" He didn't even have the decency to move on, to ask another student. I didn't want to speak to him. Ever.

But he wasn't going to let me off. All right, I thought, biting my lip again, if he wants to pretend everything's the same, fine. I could play that game in class. I'd not shown one ounce of courage on Friday, running from this room without a shred of dignity; I didn't have to sit today like a scared rabbit.

Tasting blood in my mouth, I looked directly at Mr. Dolsey. "The sentence is incorrect," I said, "because the father in the sentence is not ten years old. The sentence should read, 'Although only ten years old, I was expected to —'"

"Fine," he interrupted. "Read the next sentence, Brian," he said. He walked to the other side of the room and stood beside Brian.

I was stunned by how quickly and easily he had settled this class into work as usual. He didn't seem the slightest bit nervous. Bitterness and resentment burned in my chest; maybe *he* could go on with the daily routine, but everything was messed up for me. I didn't know how to get better grades when I couldn't even talk with him now, and I didn't know how I'd deal with my confusion in this class every day, either. The splotches on my arms turned even darker. Why'd *I* have to get stuck with this teacher? It wasn't fair!

My mind drifted to a hot afternoon a little over a year ago. Mr. Hadley had driven us over to the mine so Mama could go to the payroll department and pick up Daddy's last check. That day, a Friday in August, all four of us kids rode in the back seat of the old car. As we approached the mine entrance, hundreds of men came running up out of the shaft, heading for their cars and trucks. Wiping coal soot from their necks and faces, they laughed and hollered at one another. They acted like nothing had happened, but Daddy was no longer with them, and our whole world had been shattered. That was the day Mama broke, the only time she lost control in front of us kids.

"David's gone forever and the world goes on exactly the same!" Mama pounded her fist on the dashboard.

"Now, now, Becky," old Mr. Hadley said as he pulled into the parking area. He reached over and patted her shoulder.

Mama bent her head over into her lap, her whole body shaking with sobs. While June and Molly huddled together in the middle of the back seat, Cindy Lou reached across them and squeezed my hand tightly.

"The world doesn't even care!" Mama cried. "It's not fair! It's not fair!"

Shaking my head, I pulled my thoughts back into the classroom as Mr. Dolsey finished reviewing the requirements for our fourth paper, a book report due on Friday. Then he handed out mimeographed sheets: a pop quiz on dangling modifiers. "Write your answers on your own paper," he said, "and return the mimeographed sheets to me at the end of the hour."

Students ripped paper noisily from notebooks and pulled pencils out of pockets and purses. Finally, most heads bent over the quizzes and the room was quiet. Patricia pulled out her compact and finished off her bottom lip. She smiled at me. I smiled back.

The quiz was easy. Mr. Dolsey couldn't give me a C on something that was completely error-free. I finished the quiz quickly and stared at the books and magazines again. I wasn't going to take another C from him on essays, either. Not if I didn't really deserve it. "I'm going to stay up all night tonight," I whispered under my breath. "And the next three nights, too. The paper I turn in on Friday is going to be perfect." If Mr. Dolsey gave me one more bad grade, I'd take all my essays to the principal and ask him to read them. He could tell me if he thought every single one deserved a C.

Chapter 9

IN HOMEROOM on Thursday, the tall, skinny boy, Bobby, had a stack of newspapers, smaller than regular papers, folded in half and piled on his desk. Passing by them on my way to my seat, I saw the title, *Crabber Junior*, on the top of the front page. Mattie had said the high school kids called themselves the Crabbers. This had to be the first edition of the junior high paper. Norman's column would be in it!

Bobby was selling the papers. When Roberta gave him three dimes for one, my heart sank as I realized I didn't have any money. Roberta took her copy, slouched in the seat next to mine, and started turning the pages. Since Bobby sits right in front of Roberta, the papers weren't far from me; I leaned forward and glanced at the top one on Bobby's stack, wondering how often *Crabber Junior* came out. This one was dated October 6.

"Today's date," I muttered.

Roberta turned toward me. "Aren't you going to buy one?"

Then Bobby turned toward me, too.

"Are you on the paper staff?" I asked him quickly, hoping to draw attention from Roberta's question.

"Circulation," Bobby said. "Wanna buy one?"

"No thanks."

"Suit yourself." He picked up the stack of papers and began to parade up and down the aisles with them.

Bobby probably thought I wasn't even interested. If he only knew! So what if I'd seen Norman talking with some girl? Mattie told me flat out that Norman didn't have *girl*friends. His sister might be wrong about Norman being shy, but wouldn't she know if he had a girlfriend? That girl in the hall was probably just a friend friend. I could always hope.

"Get your Crab-ber June-yer here!" Bobby called from the first aisle.

"Not so loud, Bobby," the teacher said firmly.

The first person through the library door fourth period was Mary Fred Pratley. I went straight to the circulation desk.

"Excuse me," I said to the woman behind the long counter. "Is there a library copy of *Crabber Junior*?"

"Yes. But you have to sign for it and you can't take it out of the library." She handed me the card to sign.

"Is this the first edition this year?"

"No. The paper comes out once a month."

"Do you have the September issue?"

"We don't keep back issues."

"In my homeroom, the person from circulation on the newspaper didn't sell an issue in September."

"I'm sorry, honey. One of your friends might have one. Or you could ask someone on the paper staff. Or the faculty advisor. That's Mr. Kaufman."

"Thank you," I said as she handed me the paper. I took it to the nearest table. Leafing through the pages rapidly, I found Norman's column on page 4. It was called "Around the Bay."

His picture was at the top of the column! I moved to a table closer to the windows. Since the picture was in black and white, Norman's sandy hair looked dark. Otherwise, the picture was a perfect likeness and therefore absolutely spectacular. Wow, was he gorgeous!

I read the column fast. Norman's article was about crabbing in the Chesapeake Bay. He said that in the United States, only salmon, tuna, and shrimp are more valuable seafood catches than crabs. Americans eat more crabmeat than any other people in the world. An average of 300 million pounds of crabs are caught every year in the United States; on the market, they're worth about 80 million dollars!

I could hardly wait to tell Uncle Mack about this article; he'd be really interested. I stopped reading and looked at Norman's picture again. Then I remembered Uncle Mack's sooks scrambling in the tub on the porch. Norman wrote about "seafood catches" with admiration. How could I admire the watermen, though, if I didn't like what they did? Suddenly, I smiled at myself. I wouldn't watch Uncle Mack and Aunt Louise steam the crabs, but I'd helped pick the meat the next day. I ate some, too, and thought it was delicious.

The rest of Norman's column was about small boats — he referred to them as "small craft" — that are, in Norman's words, "indigenous to the Chesapeake Bay area because of the difficulty in getting to the shoal areas where crabs often go." Boy, Norman had an impressive vocabulary! I'd have to look up "indigenous"; I thought it meant something that belongs naturally in a certain environment. I didn't have the slightest idea what "shoal" meant.

At the end of Norman's article, he listed three books with more information on crabs. I wrote down the titles. My stomach started growling, so I returned the newspaper to the lady at the desk and took my bag lunch to the girls' room. You're not allowed to eat in the library. You're not supposed to eat in the bathroom, either, but I didn't want to fight the crowd in the cafeteria just to get milk. I wanted to get back to the library and find the three books Norman had listed; I wouldn't have much time and the last thing I needed was to be late for Mr. Dolsey's class. Since Monday when he asked me to correct that one sentence, he hadn't called on me again. I never raised my hand to volunteer an answer, either. And I didn't want to call his attention to myself by going in late.

As I hurried back to the library, I looked up to see Roberta, Jeannie, and two other girls laughing and talking. Straight across from the library doors! I'd have to walk right past them to enter. No way! I ducked into a stairwell.

Why weren't Roberta and her friends in the cafeteria? They must have finished early. I ran up the steps and rapidly crossed the whole length of the upstairs hallway. Coming back down on the other side of the building, I headed for the doors on the opposite end of the library. I'd lost five whole minutes just to avoid Roberta.

Back inside the library, I went to the card catalogue. The library didn't have one of the books Norman had mentioned and another was checked out, but I got the third one and sat down to read. I found information in the book that Norman had used for his column. The most interesting part, though, was about how blue crabs mate and reproduce. I decided crabs must be the most romantic creatures in the world! The male blue crab — the one Mattie and Aunt Louise had called a Jimmie — picks up the female so she's facing him. On his walking legs, he travels with her for two or three days, carrying her underneath him. Marine biologists call that

94

"cradle carrying" and the watermen around the Chesapeake call the couple "doublers" or "a buck and a rider."

The Jimmie looks for hiding places like eelgrass and then uses his body to make a protective cage around the female until her final moult. After they mate, the Jimmie cradle carries his sook a few more days while her final shell hardens. Then the sook can defend herself as she travels toward the lower end of the bay where she reproduces the next spring. Uncle Mack had told me about that.

The bell for the end of lunch hour rang. I read faster. The book said that if the weather turns suddenly and sharply cold while the sook's migrating, she can scurry along at amazing speeds. Some sooks travel thirty miles or more in forty-eight hours.

I closed the book, put it back on the shelf, and ran to English. I made it just as the late bell rang.

My English paper was due fifth period on Friday. I wrote my book report on a biography of Margaret Bourke-White, a famous photographer for *Look* and *Life* magazines. *Life* sent her to India to photograph Mahatma Gandhi; she loved India and stayed there. I read the book twice, took notes the second time, and then wrote my report. I rewrote it three times and copied the final draft in my neatest handwriting. Most nights that week, I waited until Aunt Louise and Uncle Mack fell asleep and then turned the lights on again in the front room so I could work late; they didn't like for me to lose sleep.

In homeroom on Friday morning, I barely listened to what the teacher said. Instead, I used scratch paper to write out different versions of a note I planned to attach to my book report. Finally, I got the message just the way I wanted it:

Mr. Dolsey:
I would like to understand the reasons for any grades I receive. However, I will never come to discuss my work with you again. When you return my essays, please include written comments (as you did on my first two papers) that explain the grade you give me.

Sincerely,
Mary Pratley

I turned my paper in to Mr. Dolsey with the note as the top page. Then I started wondering whether that was the right thing to do. I worried about it all afternoon.

When I got home from school, Aunt Louise was raking leaves in the front yard. "You sure do get a lot of mail," she said. "There are two letters for you on the table in the kitchen."

I ran inside and grabbed the letters, one from Mama and one from Cindy Lou. I took them out on the porch. The letter from Mama was cheerful like all her letters to me. She said she was amazed at how much Cindy Lou's attitude about schoolwork had changed since she got in Mrs. Swiggett's class. "Like you," Mama wrote, "Cindy Lou's growing up."

Mama mentioned briefly that Mr. Hadley was real sick. She didn't know exactly what was wrong with him but she felt certain he was "way more sick than he lets on." When she pressed him about it, he only told her that he had an appointment to see a heart specialist in a week.

The most exciting news from Mama was in the last paragraph:

Even Mr. Hadley feeling poorly, he insists on being out and about. So, guess what? He's teaching me to drive! I set my head on the idea that what with June in kindergarten now, there ain't no reason I can't find myself a job and Mr. Hadley says I can take his car coming and going to some kind of work. Days he needs the car, he'll drive me to my job and come back for me. That man's kindness knows no end.

Mama closed her letter like always by saying she loved me and for me to write soon. She underlined "write soon" – she always does that, too. This time, though, she added a P.S.:

P.S. I got a little money from the coal mine when your father died, but I been hoarding that careful for the future for you kids. If I can find work now, things'll look up pretty good, but I'm nervous as a cat, honey. I ain't worked for so long. I'm putting in applications to different places to do bookkeeping. After all these years, they still got a record on me over at the mines and a nice man there said they'll give me a reference! You be crossing your fingers for me, Mary Fred. I been thinking ever since you left as how I got to brave it out and make a new life for me, too. I'm no old woman, you know.

Mama drew a smiley face at the bottom of the page. I smiled back at the face. "Way to go!" I said out loud to it.

Mama's letters and Cindy Lou's always made me picture what they were doing and miss them. But the days I got no mail, I missed them even more. I wasn't sorry I was here; I guess I just wanted to be two places at once. I hadn't planned on feeling that. Well, there were a lot of things I hadn't planned for here, I thought as I tore open Cindy Lou's envelope.

All the joy Mama's letter brought me vanished in a flash when I read the pages from Cindy Lou. It was the longest letter I ever got from her and when I finished reading it, I had one more thing to worry about.

Dear Mary Fred,

Excuse me if I don't express myself clear. If I mess up verbs and don't use proper grammar, you can figure it's not on account of me being dumb but on account of me being so riled up I can't think straight. It's a good thing for you you wasn't here when I found out how low-down you can be.

Yesterday, coming up the road from the school bus stop, I seen Mama up on the hill staking down the wire around the chicken yard. When I got in the house, I heard little June in the bedroom clapping her hands and shouting, "Oh, you look beee-uuuu-ti-ful!" I went to the bedroom door and right there in front of my very eyes stood Molly Pratley sweeping round in your new coat!

I was hopping mad. I ran into the room and grabbed Molly's shoulders and shook her so hard I made her cry. I kept yelling at her, asking her where she got that coat. She just stared at me and set in to crying. Finally, Junie opened the closet door and climbed in under the clothes. She went back into that small storage space what opens into the closet from under the shelves in the hall. Junie said she took to playing in there a while back when she found dishes and a thimble and a scissors under there. She even found a baby's bonnet. Yesterday she pulled out an old blanket full of holes and showed it to me. She said she come upon your coat wrapped in that blanket.

I apologized to Molly for screaming at her and I made her and June promise not to tell Mama about the coat. I told them to remember that fancy word you taught them—"privy." All those weeks Mama was weaving for you, June didn't blab. I hope they're good secret-keepers. You're sure trusting on good luck that Mama don't mention the coat when she writes Aunt Louise and Uncle Mack.

Remembering the quarrel Aunt Louise and I had had about the coat, I cringed. Then I went back to Cindy Lou's letter.

It ain't no rich person's coat, but Mama can't afford no high-price store-bought one. She's learning me to weave on Mr. Hadley's loom and I see what trouble she went to for a snot what thinks she's better'n anyone else in the family.

Mama can't get no soft wool seeing as how sheep around here ain't been raised for spinners. Dowell County ain't got no bluegrass grazing areas like them up around Louisville and Lexington, so them sheep Mr. Hadley raises and shears ain't had no decent diet and they wander through the woods and knot up their wool so's they got the most tangled coats you ever seen. Mama picks and washes that wool and then she has to spend hours on end combing all those tangles out and collecting the fibers.

I found myself getting angry. Cindy Lou didn't have to tell me about those sheep; I knew what they were like. But I kept on reading.

After the spinning, Mama uses what all she's gathered for coloring and sets in on dyeing the yarn and hanging it to dry. For your coat, she used onion skins for the orange color, bark for the yellow, and rhododendron leaves for the green-gray. She soaked her leaves, plants, tree bark, and such in rainwater, then boiled them, then simmered them to get the dye. She done that separate for ever color she wanted and she put in added effort getting that beautiful rust-gold color for you, Mary Fred. She walked to Lowman's and bought alum for simmering some of the yarn in before she added it to the dye from the onion skins. That's what made the special brightness of the orange color.

The last and hardest part of weaving is getting the loom set up and fixing the warp and securing it in the loom. Right now, Mama's showing me how to thread the warp for the pattern. Soon's I learn to tie the loom, I'll be ready to try weaving.

Mama put in weeks to make that coat. She sewed a layer of burlap under the cotton sateen, too, so's it'd be extra special warm. It's a beautiful thing, but may not be splendid enough for you. You think it's nothing because you ain't got common sense for all your book learning.

After I got done talking with Molly and June, I wrapped that old blanket back around the coat and crawled into the closet. I pushed the coat into its hiding place again. I spent most of last night stewing about it and I been mad all day today at school, too. Getting this letter wrote ain't been easy, me watching all the time so's to keep Mrs. Swiggett and the other teachers what comes to our room from seeing I ain't been paying attention. Writing out this letter in little bits and pieces like I been doing kept me thinking on what you done ever hour, so's I stayed mad the whole day long.

I don't think you care a blame thing about nobody but yourself, Mary Fred. I'm probably going to stay riled up about this a long time, so maybe you just better stay away from me.

Cindy Lou didn't even sign her name to the letter. I sat holding it in my lap for a long time. Then I went inside and put it in the back of one of my notebooks. Did Cindy Lou tell Mrs. Swiggett I'd left the coat in Kentucky? Was that why Mrs. Swiggett wrote all those things about how I should appreciate Mama? No, she wrote her letter before Cindy Lou found out about the coat. Besides, Cindy Lou's not a tattletale.

After a while, I went outside to help Aunt Louise with the leaves.

"Mama's learning to drive," I said as Aunt Louise scooped big rakefuls of leaves into the plastic bag I held open. "And she's looking for a job!"

"I know. I got a letter from her today, too." Aunt Louise smiled. "I'm really proud of her. Mack will be, too, when he hears."

"The other letter was from Cindy Lou," I said.

"I noticed that — from the return address. She has beautiful handwriting."

"Yeah, but what she writes with it is practically illiterate."

"Mary Fred!" Aunt Louise shoved more leaves into the bag, using her hands this time.

"She thinks she's so great," I said.

Aunt Louise ignored that. "What'd your sister have to say?" she asked.

"A lot of things about how . . ." I closed the top of the bag and sealed it with a twist tie. "About how she's so good and everyone else is a selfish snot." I picked up the rake and slashed it through a pile of leaves.

Trying to stay busy all weekend so I wouldn't think about Cindy Lou's letter, I went grocery shopping with Uncle Mack on Saturday morning and to the laundromat with Aunt Louise on Saturday afternoon. When Aunt Louise and I got home, I decided to call Mattie.

I'd almost never made a telephone call, so the idea made me nervous. Out in the front room, I fumbled around in the phone book until I found a Garrett on our street and then I dialed the number.

"Hello," Norman said.

Oh, I was dumb! Why hadn't I anticipated this and planned what to say if *he* answered?

"Hello?" he said again.

"This is Mary Pratley," I sputtered. "May I speak to Mattie?"

"Hi, Mary!" he said in a voice so friendly it surprised me. I'd been almost rude to him Monday when I saw him talking to that girl; I figured he'd think I didn't even like him.

"Mattie went to our grandparents' for the weekend," Norman said.

"Oh." Since he sounded friendly, I didn't really want to hang up, but what could I say that was interesting? I had to think fast. His column! "I read your article about crabs," I said.

"You did? Did you like it?"

"Yes. I liked it a lot. I . . ." I stopped myself just in time — I was about to tell him I read one of the books he suggested. Boy, that would have been stupid! Did I want him to think I was interested in everything he had to say about everything?

"What?" Norman asked.

"I liked it." I'd already said that! "You're a really good writer."

"Thanks! I worked on that article pretty hard. I already knew a lot about crabs from being out in Hampton Roads and on the bay with my dad. But I read books to get more information."

"Do you always write about fishing or crabbing?"

"No. I write about anything that's going on in Tidewater, but I think the paper should have a column on crabbing once a year."

"Sure. After all, it's *Crabber Junior*." I couldn't think of anything else to say to him. I pressed my fingernails into my palms.

"What've you been doing?" Norman asked, keeping the conversation going.

"Not much. I was going to ask Mattie if I could come over this afternoon and hear her play the saxophone."

"You're lucky she's not home then. She's awful."

"Oh, I bet she's not!"

"Well, I'm sorry you didn't get her. *I'm* home, though."

What did that mean?

"If you want to talk on the phone," Norman said, "I'm a lot more interesting than Mattie."

You sure are, I thought. And Norman seemed to like talking with me. But the more we talked, the more nervous I felt. I hadn't said anything *too* stupid yet and I wanted to get off the phone before I did. "I'm pretty busy now," I said, "so I have to go."

"Oh. Well, it was nice talking to you. I'm glad you like my column."

"I do. It's great."

"I'll tell Mattie you called."

"Thanks. Bye."

I hung up fast. Pretty busy? How could I be busy if I'd called to see if I could visit Mattie? That was really stupid. Stupid. Stupid.

Chapter 10

Mr. Dolsey handed back our book reports at the end of the period the next Thursday. The note I'd written him was still attached to the front of my paper.

Walking down the hall to my next class, I leafed through the pages to the last one; from the bottom left corner, a small letter in dark black ink jumped up to slap me: C. Underneath it, there was a brief note: "Grammar flawless. Diction poor — too verbose. I think we should talk again, Mary. Please make an appointment with me."

No way! I'd never go talk with him alone again! Didn't he even read my note?

Whirling around, I bumped into two boys behind me as I started in the opposite direction. He hadn't written a single remark about the content. Didn't the *content* count? I raced to the office. Inside, I walked straight to the desk of the secretary who'd taken me to my homeroom on my first day in the school.

"Ma'am," I said, "I'd like to make an appointment to see the principal. If possible, I'd like to come tomorrow."

I had mail again that afternoon. The envelope with Mama's handwriting pleased me; I hadn't heard from her for nearly a week and I needed something to turn my mind from worry over the next morning. The principal would never take my word if I accused Mr. Dolsey. Should I just talk about the grades? What Mr. Dolsey had done, though – didn't that have something to do with the grades?

I turned Mama's letter over and over. What he'd done was wrong! The principal should know.

Mama's letter felt good in my hands. I opened it and read it at the kitchen table.

Dear Mary Fred.

I'm making this short since I'm beside myself with excitement and things to do, but I want you to know that right after I wrote you last week – the very next day – I got a job! And this morning I got another one!

I give Mr. Hadley's phone number at the places where I asked for work. Thursday a call come through from that new brass mill on the other side of Tyler. They left a message for me to come that afternoon for an interview. Mr. Hadley took me and they give me the job! I'll work half days five days a week. It's mostly paper work – filing, entering in log books, and payroll. I start tomorrow. Wish me luck.

The next big news is that this morning a lady dressed up all fancy drove right up to the house in a big new car and come in to see me. She said she couldn't find no phone number for me so she just drove into Tyler and asked around until she found out how to find me. Turns out she lives over near the new brass mill. She's the director for the Dowell County Community Center over there. That center's for Tyler, Rollinsboro, Gatlinville, and all the towns in this county. The end of the month, they're starting up new classes for children and adults in all kinds of crafts. More folks signed up already than they planned on so they need extra teachers.

This woman – her name's Mrs. Pollard – she come here

because she'd cut out and saved that article about my wooden dolls and crafts and now she's wanting me to come over Tuesday nights and teach weaving! And Thursday nights wood carving. I told her I ain't got no car and depend on Mr. Hadley for my way to my new job. I don't feel right burdening him no more. Besides, I got three younguns here I can't leave nights. None of that even fazed her. She said she'll come get me both nights each week and bring me home seeing as how she goes to the center herself them nights. She said to bring along all the girls, too. What's more, they're going to pay me!

I just couldn't say no, honey. She was such a sweet lady and I need the money. You know how I love my craft things, anyways. I swear, Mary Fred, I'm more excited about this than about my good job that pays right decent at the brass mill. Why, when that nice Mrs. Pollard got here, I had the materials for the corn husk wreaths me and Cindy Lou'll sell for Christmas spread all over this front room—wire coat hangers, corn husks, rickrack, quilt blocks, and little bottles of glue. I couldn't hardly find no place for that lady to sit and she didn't seem to mind the least bit; matter of fact, I think that cinched the job for me—ha!

This turned out to be a fair piece of writing for somebody started out saying as how they'd be sending a short letter. You can share it with Louise and Mack so they'll know my news—I ain't got time to write them, too, tonight. I got to get this house cleaned up and figure out what on earth I'm going to wear to that brass plant tomorrow. I miss you, sweetheart, and I love you. *Write me soon.*

Mama

P.S. I'm going to splurge on one thing what with me having some income now. I'm getting us a telephone put in. Cindy Lou's beside herself excited. We'll celebrate when it's in here by giving you a call. Maybe by sometime next week. Bye again.

"Aunt Louise!" I hollered. "Where are you?"

106

"I'm on the porch, honey."

I ran out there. "Oh, that's pretty," I said, noticing the bright green yarn on her lap. Her knitting needles were flying.

"I'm starting a sweater for Mack for Christmas," she said. "Don't tell him."

I sat down on the glider beside her. "Wait'll you hear this letter from Mama!"

The next morning, the secretary left me in a chair beside an enormous wooden desk in the principal's office. "You should only have to wait a minute or two," she said.

Through a big window, sunlight fell across books, magazines, folders, and stacks of papers on the desk. Pens and pencils were scattered everywhere. Looking out the window, I saw the same chain link fence I'd run into in confusion after my meeting with Mr. Dolsey.

A copy of *Crabber Junior* was folded in half on the corner of the desk. I picked it up. Last Thursday's paper. I was turning to page 4 — to see Norman's picture again — when I heard someone come into the room.

"Good morning," a woman's voice said behind me. "Are you Mary Pratley?"

"Yes."

"What can I do for you?"

"I'm waiting to see the principal."

The lady smiled and wrinkles bunched around her eyes, bright blue eyes even clearer than Daddy's were. "I'm the principal, Mary," she said and seated herself in a big leather-covered chair behind the desk.

"Oh." I tried not to stare, but she was so pretty. Gray strands in her curly black hair threw off small flashes of light in the sun. Her face had soft skin like Mama's with the same flush on her cheeks that Mama has when she's been working outside. She wore an elegant dress, the light blue wool the color of her eyes and the high collar up to her chin.

"I'm Mrs. Crider," she said. "You wanted to talk with me?"

I'd practiced my words half the night before and all the way to school, but I couldn't remember how I was supposed to begin. I closed the newspaper on my lap, folded it, and put it back on the desk. Then I stared at Mrs. Crider's sleeves, full at the top, closed tightly around her small wrists.

"Mary?"

I looked up.

"Is it about Mr. Dolsey and your English class?" she asked.

"What?" How could she know about that? "Ma'am?"

"Mr. Dolsey mentioned you to me a few days ago. He said that you might complain about your grades." She settled herself back in her chair. "Mr. Dolsey feels that, since you come from a poorer area of the country with somewhat inferior schools, it's inevitable that your performance here would be only average for a while. Does that seem a fair assessment to you?"

"No, ma'am!" I bit my bottom lip. I couldn't believe Mr. Dolsey had taken advantage of the things I'd told him and used them to invent a story to make himself look innocent.

"The expectations here *are* high, Mary," Mrs. Crider said, "but I'm sure that you'll do well if you work hard and are patient. It may take a little time to adjust, that's all."

"My school in Kentucky wasn't good in several areas," I said, "but I had a great English teacher last year and I had her for sixth- and seventh-grade English, too. I think my writing's clear and correct. I know I can improve, but . . ." I hesitated.

"Yes? Go on," Mrs. Crider said.

Talking slowly, I told her about Mrs. Swiggett, about my

reading and writing, and about my desire to become a teacher. I explained how hard I had worked on my first three papers and that, after giving me three Cs, Mr. Dolsey had asked me to come for a conference.

"What did he tell you?" Mrs. Crider asked.

I leaned forward and gripped one corner of the desk tightly. Telling Mrs. Crider was going to be even harder than I'd thought. But I had to do it. I looked up into her friendly eyes. I had to trust her.

"Mary? What did he say?"

I straightened my back and kept my grip on the desk. "It's not what he said." I took a deep breath. Talking faster and louder as I got more nervous, I told her everything about the conference in Mr. Dolsey's classroom after school. When I got to the part about Mr. Dolsey touching me, I kept my eyes on the floor until I'd finished.

"I see," Mrs. Crider said. She turned her chair away from me and gazed out the window. "I see," she said again.

After a minute she turned back to me. "Mr. Dolsey's been here only a year. This fall he's beginning his second year with us. He came to Hampton with good references — after twenty-four years of teaching in Cleveland — to be near his elderly parents who are ill. That's very commendable, don't you think, Mary?"

I didn't understand her point, but I nodded.

"No one has ever complained about him."

"But if he's only been here a year —"

"In that one year, he's done many fine things in this community. And he's proven himself to be an excellent teacher." Mrs. Crider pushed her hand under one stack of papers after another until she found a pack of cigarettes. She kept her fingers on the pack and looked at me again. "I'm not saying

I don't believe you. But I have to be careful. I have to . . ."
She stopped.

"After what happened," I said, "I put a note on my fourth
paper asking him to write comments explaining my grades.
He didn't, though. He gave me another C and wrote on the
paper that we should talk again. I was so mad that I decided
to come to you."

"I'm glad you did. Have you discussed this matter with
anyone else?"

"No, ma'am." I pulled out my essays. "Mrs. Crider, will
you read these and see if you think they've been graded fairly?"
I handed them across the desk to her. "And, ma'am, if you'd
talk with my other teachers, I think they'd tell you I can do
good work here. I haven't made a grade less than B in any
other class."

Mrs. Crider pushed the pack of cigarettes down into an
empty ashtray under some folders. "I've got to quit smoking,"
she said to the ashtray. Then she stood up. "All right, Mary,"
she said. "I'll read your papers."

"Thank you."

She walked around to my side of the desk, still holding the
essays in one hand. "I can't, of course, ask you not to mention
this situation to your family. Actually, it . . ." She sighed.
"It would be best if you *did* inform your aunt and uncle.
However, I'd appreciate it if you would not discuss it here at
the school."

"I won't."

"I'll be in touch with you when I've had time to consider
the matter carefully."

"Yes, ma'am. Thank you for seeing me."

"Do you have your own copy of *Crabber Junior*?" she asked
suddenly, picking up the paper.

"No, ma'am. I read it in the library."

"Would you like this one? I have another at home." She handed it to me before I could even say yes.

"Thank you!" I said. As I picked up my books, I saw Mrs. Crider drop my essays onto her desk. She'd probably never read them; she wouldn't even be able to find them again.

"Goodbye," I said and left the office quickly. I didn't think Mrs. Crider believed a thing I'd told her about Mr. Dolsey.

From the kitchen, Aunt Louise called out to me as I came through the front door that afternoon.

"Mary Fred? Hurry in here, honey. You got a package today. Huge! It's postmarked Tyler, Kentucky, but it's not from your mama."

I looked at the big box. It was wrapped in brown grocery bag paper, the same way Mama wraps all her packages. The return address, printed in block letters, said "Luther Hadley." Mr. Hadley? Why would Mr. Hadley send me a package?

Aunt Louise handed me a knife and I cut the string and tore off the paper. On top of the box were two sheets of notebook paper. Cindy Lou's handwriting. What was going on? I used the knife to slice through the tape around the box. Opening the carton, I pulled out some newspapers wrapped around the contents. My heart skipped about ten beats.

I saw Aunt Louise's eyes narrow in surprise, but she turned away quietly and opened the refrigerator door. "I better start figuring out what we're going to eat tonight," she said.

I picked up Cindy Lou's letter, took it into the front room and read it alone.

Dear Mary Fred,
    I finally settled on what to do about the coat. I couldn't take one single chance on Mama poking around in that

closet space to find something she wants, so the only thing was to get the coat away from the house. This morning I chose careful what minute to leave so's I went out the door without Mama seeing the coat bunched in with my books. I had to carry it around all day.

After school, I got off the bus down the road from Mr. Hadley's and went straight to his place. I told him the whole story. Blamed if he didn't take up for you, saying as how you're proud and that's only a human weakness. Then he went on about how when we're young sometimes we do things we regret later but that's human, too. It made me want to puke to hear him make excuses for you, especially when you think he's a strange old fogey and don't even like him.

I asked Mr. Hadley to box the coat and, beings I ain't got no money, I had to shame myself begging him to pay the postage on it next time he goes to town. I never in my life asked nobody for money, but I didn't have no choice. I felt even worse seeing as how Mr. Hadley ain't been feeling good — he don't even seem to breathe right — but he said he's going in to the doctor tomorrow and wouldn't mind at all to mail it. I'm sitting at his table now, writing this letter to leave for him to put in the package. Mama won't know I been here. I always come home late Tuesdays because of my Tri-Hi-Y meeting, but I had to skip it today so I could take care of this — there's another reason for me being riled up at you.

You probably wanted Aunt Louise and Uncle Mack to buy you a fancy ski jacket, so you'll be put out when the box comes and they know you left behind such a fine coat. They'll see you don't take no pride in all the work Mama done. I don't even know if you take pride in Mama. But you best be asking Aunt Louise and Uncle Mack not to tell her about you leaving the coat here.

Cindy Lou

My sister was getting good at preaching sermons at me; I guess she was feeling pretty proud of herself because she even bothered to sign her name this time.

I shoved the letter into the same notebook with the other one and went back to the kitchen. Picking up the coat, I flinched at the sight of the bright yellow and orange stripes. Maybe the coat wouldn't have been *so* bad if Mama hadn't gone to all that extra work, using the alum to heighten the color. The green-gray was right pretty, a nice shade for red-heads. Why didn't she make the whole coat that color?

Carrying the coat into the bathroom, I closed the door. I tried it on and looked in the mirror. The morbid lining didn't really matter, I thought. No one could see that. The hand-knitted cuffs weren't noticeable, either, unless I held up my arms, and I knew they'd be snug and warm. Kids wouldn't notice things like the lining or the cuffs. And the coat's slightly oversized fit didn't make it look as obviously homemade as I'd first thought—I was probably being entirely too picky. I had to admit Cindy Lou was right that Mama did nice work. But that bright orange . . . I'd be just too conspicuous. I couldn't wear it.

I crossed through the kitchen and hung the coat up in the corner of the closet by the front door where I kept all my things. Aunt Louise didn't say anything, but something in her eyes told me what I already knew: I was a coward. The weather was turning colder, just as she had said, but I didn't have the courage to face anyone who might tease me if I wore the coat. And I was even afraid of something as simple as taking Cindy Lou's advice and asking my aunt and uncle not to tell Mama I'd left the coat in Kentucky. I didn't want to hear what they'd say about me if I brought up the topic, so I remained silent and trusted that their kindness would keep them from mentioning it to Mama. Most cowardly of all, though, was my decision not to follow Mrs. Crider's advice about telling Aunt Louise and Uncle Mack what Mr. Dolsey had done.

Feeling miserable, I avoided Aunt Louise's eyes the whole evening. I kept everything to myself.

Chapter 11

Aunt Louise and Uncle Mack decided I could buy my lunch once a week. I chose Tuesdays. On the Tuesday after my Friday meeting with Mrs. Crider, I stopped at the library during the first part of my lunch hour. When I got to the cafeteria, the line was short. Almost everybody was already eating. After receiving the standard lunch — a slab of ham, string beans, half a peach on lettuce, a slice of bread, and a carton of milk — I carried my tray to one end of a crowded table. I wished Mattie had lunch hour with me. I hated eating alone. Pulling out a chair and sitting, I heard Roberta's voice only two or three seats down from me.

"Mary Ph-red Pa-RAT-ley is he-ah today. He-ah, ma-am."

I opened my carton of milk and drank some.

Roberta went on. "My daddy says this whole town's being taken over by them hillbillies coming in here and grabbing up all the jobs in the shipyard. Your daddy work in the shipyard, Ph-red?"

I looked down at my tray and picked up a napkin. I'd forgotten silverware.

Roberta's voice grew louder. "Daddy says the hillnellies

stand around in the grocery stores just staring 'cause they don't even know what to buy. Them hayseeds ain't never eat nothing but cornbread and grits."

All the kids at Roberta's end of the table laughed.

I walked quickly to the bins of knives, forks, and spoons at the back of the lunch line. A throbbing in my head made me feel faint. Breathing deeply to fight the dizziness, I heard my aunt Louise's voice: "You are what you think you are." I stood tall, pulled my shoulders back, and concentrated on walking gracefully as I went back to my seat at the lunch table.

"Hey, Ph-red," a black-haired girl hollered from the other end of the table. "Ain't you scared you going to get sick eating that city food?"

I glanced at the girl. It was Jeannie Johnston, my homeroom's new representative to student council.

"Why didn't you bring your lunch in a sack today?" Jeannie yelled. "Bring us all some cornbread and black-eyed peas tomorrow, O.K.?"

My eyes ached from the pain in my head. I felt my left eyelid start to twitch.

"My daddy says they ought not to let them briar-hoppers go to school in the cities," Roberta shrilled. "They bring in cooties from up in the hills. Your folks from the hills, Ph-red?"

I wasn't going to talk to them and I wasn't going to cry. Glancing around the room, I saw an empty seat at the next table. I stood, picked up my tray, and walked past Roberta and Jeannie. My vision blurred a little as I saw Bobby, two seats beyond them, tipping his chair up on its back legs.

"How come you don't buy *Crabber Junior*, Ph-red?" he asked. "Hillbillies can't read?" Suddenly, Bobby's chair tilted

116

farther than he'd planned; it started to go over backward. Frantically, he threw himself forward, grabbing the edge of the table as the front legs of the chair slammed to the floor.

Everything in the cafeteria began to whirl around me and I tripped on one of the chair legs. I fell, my tray crashing in front of me. Dishes and utensils clattered across the linoleum. My nose struck the corner of the tray sharply and began to bleed. As I pulled myself up to my knees and wiped the blood onto my hand, I saw the white stockings of one of the ladies who works in the cafeteria."

"What's going on here?" the woman asked, taking hold of my elbow and helping me to my feet.

"Thank you," I mumbled. I brushed past her quickly and ran from the cafeteria.

"My, ain't them ridge-runners clumsy?" Jeannie yelled after me amidst the laughter of the other kids.

Racing toward the front entrance of the school, I wiped my nose again. I couldn't stay for the rest of the day. Crying. Humiliated. Blood all over the front of Cindy Lou's sweater. As I approached the front door, I saw Mr. Dolsey coming toward me. This wasn't happening! Not today! I walked faster and pretended to look in another direction.

Mr. Dolsey walked right up to me. "What happened to you, Mary?" he asked.

The bell rang for the end of fourth-period lunch and the hammering in my head began again.

"Mary? What happened to your nose? Are you all right?"

I tried to step around Mr. Dolsey but he stayed with me.

"Maybe you should see the school nurse. What happened?"

"I don't want to talk to you," I said, heading toward the door again.

"Are you all right?"

He wasn't going to leave me alone! "No!" I spat the word at him. "I'm not all right!"

"What happened? What's wrong?"

"Everything's wrong!" I pressed the palm of my hand against my forehead, trying to push away the pain. "All of you, you and Roberta and Jeannie —"

"You talked with Roberta?" Mr. Dolsey stopped abruptly between me and the door. "What did Roberta tell you?"

"What're you talking about? She's a creep!" I shouted. "All of you think I'm nothing. You treat me like dirt —"

"Mary! Please." Mr. Dolsey's eyes darted around the hallway. Students raced up and down the corridor, slamming locker doors, hollering at one another, heading for fifth period. A tall boy separated himself from one group of kids and moved in our direction. It was Norman! I didn't believe it! How could everything go wrong at once like this?

"Please calm down," Mr. Dolsey said. "I think we need to talk about your grades and about —"

"About what you did to me?"

"Mary, I didn't mean —"

"You liar! You talked to me like I was cheap. Where I come from, nobody talks to anyone like that, asking dirty, ugly questions . . ."

I stopped. Norman was standing in front of me. I looked down at the floor, but I had no way to hide my tears or the blood.

"Hi," he said. Then he saw my face. "Mary! What *happened* to you?"

Naturally, my nose chose that very minute to start bleeding like crazy again. Why'd I have to run into Norman when my face looked like a boxer's right after he loses a fifteen-round fight?

"I fell and hurt myself," I managed to say. My head felt ready to explode.

"How?"

"I dropped my tray in the cafeteria and hit my nose on it when I fell." I wiped the back of my hand across my nose.

Mr. Dolsey took a handkerchief from his pocket and held it out to me. I ignored him.

"Are you all right?" Norman asked.

I nodded.

Mr. Dolsey held the handkerchief out to me again.

"Keep it!" I said. "I don't want it!"

Norman looked stunned.

"I have to go home now," I said.

"I'll walk you," Norman said.

"No!" I said over my shoulder. Oh, you jerk, I thought—now Norman's *really* going to think you don't like him; first you're rude to him in the hall, then you practically hang up on him on the phone, and you top that off by snapping at him when he tries to help you. "Thanks, anyway, Norman!" I called to him and went out the door.

Mr. Dolsey followed me. "Mary," he said on the brick walk in front of the school, "I'd appreciate it if you'd let me explain—"

"What's for you to explain?"

"I'm only asking you to consider—"

"Don't try to get out of it! What you did shamed me! And they—"

"Please lower your voice," Mr. Dolsey said, jerking his head toward four girls talking on the front lawn not very far from us. Students are allowed to walk around on the grounds during lunch period.

"They try to shame me, too," I said. "They —"

"Who? Tell me what's got you so upset."

"I'm not some dumb little hillbilly! All of you think I'm stupid because I'm a hillbilly!" My voice trembled, but I went on. "Did you think I'd go along with you because I want good grades?"

"Mary! The grades you received had nothing . . . Your work *does* need improvement. I'd like for us to sit down and talk about it seriously."

"I don't want to talk to you about my grades. I don't want to talk to you about anything!"

"You can still get good grades, Mary, if —"

"If I go along with your creepy —"

"That is *not* what I mean."

The bell for fifth period rang.

"I don't care what you mean!" I said. I could hear the pounding in my head now. "It's not fair for you —"

"Mary, please show some regard for my position. People can hear you." He stepped off the walk and onto the grass as the group of four girls moved toward the front door. One of them stared at him and then looked back at me. Several students ran from other parts of the lawn to the building.

"You didn't show any regard for me!" I said, raising my voice.

Mr. Dolsey walked quickly back to me. "Can you wait until the students are inside the —"

"And it's not fair for you to try to talk with me about all this. You should talk with Mrs. Crider!" I started toward the sidewalk by the street.

Mr. Dolsey followed me to the end of the brick walk.

"Mrs. Crider told me this morning that she'd read your papers," he said. "She feels I graded them somewhat harshly but I want you to understand that I certainly did not intentionally —"

"I told her what you did." I walked away from him.

"I'm not sure that talking with Mrs. Crider was the wisest thing to do." I could hear the quiver in his voice. "I wish you hadn't done that."

I whirled back around. "Am I supposed to just let you ruin my life here? You and Roberta and all her friends!" I could barely breathe. "Well, I won't let you! I—" For a minute, I couldn't talk at all. I started crying, then sobbing.

"You're bullies!" I shouted through the sobs. "You push me around, treat me like dirt, make me feel like nothing!" My breath came in gasps and my chest hurt so bad that I bent over, sobbing harder. "Please leave me alone!"

Mr. Dolsey reached over and put his hand on my shoulder.

I jerked my body out from under his fingers. "Don't touch me!" I screamed, stumbling backward. When I caught my balance and stood up straight, I saw a glaze of tears over Mr. Dolsey's big blue eyes. He stood holding his hand in midair, staring at it, and suddenly I realized he hadn't touched me the way he had before, after school. He'd reached out to comfort me like . . . like a father.

"Mary," he said, helplessness in his eyes, "I didn't realize this whole . . . this . . . incident . . . would be so . . . I need you to understand . . ."

I hated him for making me feel so confused! I didn't *want* to feel sorry for him!

"I have to go," I said, turning away.

"Your life here's not ruined," he said quietly behind me.

I kept my eyes ahead of me and ran down the street. Was

that all I could do? Run? Run from Mr. Dolsey. Run from the cafeteria with a tear-stained face when those snotty kids needed to be stood up to. Feeling completely sorry for myself, I slowed to a walk. I'd probably fail English after what I'd just done. Mrs. Crider wasn't going to help me, either; "somewhat harshly" was all she'd told Mr. Dolsey about my grades. Hadn't she even mentioned the other things I'd told her? And I didn't belong in this big city; none of these city kids liked me. Except Mattie. And perhaps Norman. Just perhaps.

Maybe I should have stayed in Kentucky where I did belong. Nobody there was as mean and hateful as these kids. Even the daughters of the coal mine operators back home, the rich girls, never acted so rude or cruel. I hated the kids here for talking about country people the way they did, for making fun of me, for ridiculing my accent and what I had to eat.

A block from the school, I stopped at the corner to catch my breath. My nose had stopped bleeding, but tears still burned my eyes. I missed Mama and Cindy Lou so bad. I wanted to talk to them about everything. But Cindy Lou was furious with me. She did me a favor, getting that coat mailed. And I deserved the letter she sent with it — the one before that, too. She wouldn't even want to see me now. And Mama'd be so hurt if she found out what I'd done. She probably wouldn't want to talk with me, either. I thought about the sooks and the Jimmies; I wished I had someone to hold me while I grew strong.

I crossed the street and started down the next block. Feeling homesick and lonesome wasn't going to do me any good, I thought. Obviously, I couldn't be with Mama or Cindy Lou today. Why hadn't I gone over to visit Mattie so I'd have a friend? I'd tried to call her only one time in the three weeks since the night we talked about Roberta in my yard. And why'd I just sit around by myself in the cafeteria and in my classes, waiting for everyone to come to me? Did I think everyone in the whole school was as mean as Roberta? I hadn't done a single thing to make friends.

I gazed at the blood on Cindy Lou's sweater. Boy, Cindy Lou would put these city kids in their proper places and no maybes about it. I was wrong to tell Mr. Dolsey that they all made me feel like nothing. *I* was the one who made me feel like nothing. "You don't take no pride," Cindy Lou wrote me.

Go ahead and cry, I told myself. Just get all the tears out of your system right this minute because this is the end of it, Mary Fred! Mama found out life's not fair; she grieved and cried but now she's fighting. Just like Cindy Lou. Just like Aunt Louise and Uncle Mack losing their babies and trying again. Pratleys aren't quitters.

I stopped crying. Looking up, I saw four huge bags stuffed full of leaves and lined up neatly on the edge of a driveway. A fifth bag had fallen over. The seam down the side of the green plastic had split; spilling out of the bag, leaves blew down the sidewalk and onto the street. Leaning over, I set the bag upright, turning the torn side inward toward the other bags.

My headache was almost gone, but my left eyelid twitched again. At least I'd done something about Mr. Dolsey, I thought as I reached the last block on the street. Oh yeah, I'd done something, all right. I'd screamed and yelled at a teacher! But he deserved it. I rubbed my eyelid. For a moment I saw an image of Mr. Dolsey holding his hand up in the air after I screamed at him. Did I feel sorry for him now? It was easier to hate him. *Was* he sorry for what he did, though? Even if he was, I didn't know what to think about him. But I wasn't afraid anymore about the grades. High grades could carry me to good things in my life, but if Mrs. Crider didn't help me, I could live with a C in English this year. I wasn't going to swallow my pride for an A.

Passing Mattie and Norman's house, I hoped Aunt Louise would let me stay home the rest of the afternoon. I'd tell her about falling but not about the rest of the things that had happened in the cafeteria; the whole truth would worry her. I'd apologize to Aunt Louise, too, for acting so uppity the morning she'd said I needed a coat.

The wind chilled me, but I smiled. Mama said she was going to brave it out. If she could do it, I could, too. No more Miss Doormat! I walked faster toward home. Tomorrow I'd wear my coat. And just dare Roberta to say a word about it. No more running. Not from Mr. Dolsey. Not from Roberta or Jeannie or Bobby. Mary Fred Pratley would never run out of that school again.

Chapter 12

AUNT LOUISE was knitting when I got home Tuesday afternoon, Uncle Mack's sweater-to-be spread out on her lap. Sitting on the floor with her back up against the sofa bed, she had a book propped open against a stack of magazines on the coffee table. When I came in the front door, she said "Hi, Mary Fred" without even looking at me; her eyes were too busy darting back and forth between the green yarn and a page of the book.

"What're you reading?" I asked.

"Oh, it's a book about colonial America. It's so interesting! Did you know —"

Aunt Louise stopped when she glanced up and got a good look at me. She put the book and the yarn right aside and, after she heard my story, she made me wash up to go all the way downtown to a doctor.

"My nose isn't bleeding anymore," I insisted.

"I can see it's not bleeding now. But you smashed it hard — look at all that blood on your sweater. Never can tell when there's damage you can't see."

"It doesn't hurt at all."

"Get out of that sweater fast so I can do a cold-water wash. Blood sets."

In the bathroom, I washed my face, put on a clean shirt, and combed my hair. When I came back to the kitchen, Aunt Louise was rolling Cindy Lou's sweater gently in a towel to get out the excess water. She spread the sweater out to dry on a clean towel on the counter and turned off the spaghetti sauce she had simmering in a huge pot.

We took the 1:10 bus. Downtown, after we waited almost an hour, Aunt Louise's doctor assured her that my nose was fine. She didn't seem to mind at all that she'd spent money for nothing.

Back home, Aunt Louise went right to the front room to knit some more. Or to read. Or both. Sitting down with my homework at the kitchen table, I wasted half an hour thinking about all the things that had happened at school that day and stewing about the next day. Hadn't I made everything worse? If I thought that first class after what Mr. Dolsey did to me was hard to face, imagine what I was going to feel like walking into that room tomorrow. Would he try to talk to me again?

No matter how hard I tried, I couldn't concentrate. At last I closed my books and just sat there. I wanted Aunt Louise to leave the front room so I could get my coat from the closet and look at it again in the bathroom.

"Should you check the spaghetti sauce?" I called to her.

"Hmmm?"

"The spaghetti sauce."

"Just turn it back on simmer, honey."

She's going to see it anyway, I thought. I turned on the flame under the sauce, went to the front room, and took the coat from the closet. Aunt Louise didn't look up. Halfway to the bathroom, I turned around and went back to her, the coat hanging over my arm.

"I have to tell you something," I stammered.

She looked at the coat. "What, honey?"

"Remember that word you used the other day about me? Uppity."

She laughed. "That was my mama's favorite word for describing us kids when we got out of line."

"I was out of line. Plain uppity. I'm sorry, Aunt Louise."

"Don't worry about it. What's done's done." She turned her book face down on the table by the sofa. "I see you're giving thought to wearing your coat."

My face was probably the color of the orange stripes, but I put on the coat and turned around in it for her.

Aunt Louise held up her hand, palm out. "Don't fuss with me anymore now, Mary Fred, 'cause I know I'm right about this. That coat does *not* look homemade. That coat looks like Saks Fifth Avenue." She pulled some newspapers from the shelf under the lamp table. After a minute or two of turning pages, she found the fashion section of last Sunday's paper. "Look at this." She held up a page with pictures of women in wool coats. "Handwoven. On sale in the finest stores in New York. Expensive, too."

I looked at the pictures and smiled at her. "I'd already decided to wear it," I said.

"That's my girl!" She jumped up. "Come on!" she said, heading for the back of the house.

In the bedroom, Aunt Louise opened the top drawer of the chest. "Listen," she said as she scrounged around in the folded clothing in the drawer. "You don't like the fullness of the coat and you don't like the colors, right?"

"The pale green's nice."

"*All* the colors are stunning. But the green's nicest for your hair and complexion." She pulled out a long narrow scarf — an almost *perfect* match for the green-gray Mama'd gotten from the rhododendron leaves! "Put this in the neck," she said, handing me the scarf. Then she got down on her knees and began to poke through the things in the bottom drawer.

I arranged the scarf carefully. I tucked in only a little of it, leaving most of the silky material visible above the tailored collar. "That brings out the green color a lot!" I said, looking in the mirror over the chest.

She pulled something from the drawer she'd been searching, whipped it quickly behind her back, and stood up. "The scarf is yours to keep. This next thing's a loan. I made over it so when I saw it in a store window in Rollinsboro one time that Mack went back later and bought it for a birthday present for me. Cost him a pretty penny and he shouldn't have done it, but, my, I was tickled."

Aunt Louise's hand came from behind her back. In it she held the loveliest belt I ever saw — a wide, soft leather belt in a rich brown color. She put the belt around my waist and fastened the gold metal buckle. "There!" she said. "The coat won't seem quite so full. I do believe that looks plumb beautiful. And so do you."

I went to Aunt Louise and hugged her.

My locker's in the hallway outside my homeroom. Wednesday morning, I was trying to open the combination lock when the door at the top of the staircase slammed and a tall boy started down the hall. Norman! He was going to see me in the coat. My whole body went rigid. Would he say anything about my bloody nose yesterday? Or the fact that I'd been yelling at a teacher? Maybe he'd ask me why I'd gotten off the phone so fast the day I called Mattie or why I'd walked away from him so abruptly yesterday. Even worse, maybe he'd pass by without speaking at all.

"Hi, Mary," Norman said, stopping beside me.

"Hello." He *was* speaking to me!

"How're things going?"

My lock wasn't working. I swirled the dial and started over again, my hands shaking. "Fine," I said.

"That's good." Norman leaned up against the locker next to mine.

I gave up on the lock and tried to decide what to talk about with him. I couldn't just stand there gawking at his soft-colored green shirt and trying to avoid his beautiful green eyes; I didn't want him to think I was really boring.

"When's *Crabber Junior* coming out again?" I asked.

"It's supposed to be out November Third, but we're behind schedule. We're shooting for November Tenth now."

"What're you writing about this time?"

"Well, since this is November, I'm writing about the Big Brother–Big Sister Program at the high schools. Every November–"

"Hey, Garrett!" a boy yelled from the other end of the corridor. "Get a move on. You're late!"

"Keep your shirt on!" Norman yelled back at the boy. He turned to me again. "Every November, ninth-graders get assigned a Big Brother or Sister at the high school they'll attend. For the rest of that year and then when the ninth-grader enters high school, Big Brother – or Sister – teaches Little Brother or Sis about high school life and helps with the changes."

"That's a neat idea," I said.

"My column gives reasons for having a program like that

for sixth-graders coming to junior high. Or for new students. Like you."

"I think that'd be great!"

His look turned serious. "You want to join the paper staff?"

"I . . ." Norman wanted me to join the paper staff?! The idea was so unexpected that I didn't know what to say; my mouth felt as if it were clamped shut. "I . . . I don't know," I stammered.

"You said you like to write. You ought to think about it."

"I will," I said. Wouldn't I see Norman every single day if I joined the paper staff? "I'll think about it."

"Good." With one elbow, he pushed his body away from the locker. "Well, I'll be seeing you." He hesitated. "Soon, I hope," he added and took off down the hall.

Oh, I hope so, too, I thought. I couldn't believe Norman had been so nice; he hadn't mentioned my bloody nose or Mr. Dolsey or any of the times he might have thought I'd acted rude. And I didn't think he'd even noticed my coat.

I stood without moving for a second, my heart still feeling a little shaky, as Bobby ran by me. He whipped back around.

"Well, look at this!" he said. To the walls, I guess. He went down the hall to the doorway of our homeroom. "Hey, Jeannie!" he called into the room. "Come out here. Something you gotta see!"

I turned the dial on my lock again, forcing myself to concentrate on the numbers. A second later, Bobby and Jeannie came back, standing just a little way down the hall from me.

"What's today?" Bobby asked Jeannie, loud enough for me to hear.

"Wednesday."

"No, I mean the date."

"I don't know. Oh, October Nineteenth, I think."

"You sure it's October? I was thinking maybe it's December. There's our school Christmas tree right over there lighting up this whole hall."

The lock sprang open in my hand. I turned to face Bobby. "When this coat was given to me, I predicted that someone would compare it to a Christmas tree. You're probably attracted to the bright, pretty colors. Most little kids are."

"Very funny," Bobby said. He walked up and touched the back of the coat. "Ouch! Better not get your hands on this," he said over his shoulder to Jeannie. "It'll cut you."

Jeannie walked over and ran her hand across my shoulder. "You're right," she said to Bobby.

Roberta was coming down the hall toward us. "Hey, you guys!" she hollered. "What's going on?"

"We're looking at Ph-red's new costume for the Halloween party," Jeannie said. "She's going as a Christmas tree. Where'd you get the costume, Ph-red?"

"It's a gift from my mother," I said as I opened my locker door. "She made it."

"Oooh," Bobby said. "Big deal."

"Yes," I said. "It's a big deal." I put my bag lunch up on the shelf in the locker and pulled the scarf out of the neck of my coat. "My mother teaches sewing and weaving and wood carving. She's an artist."

"Well, la, dee, da," Bobby said. "She the one that makes that 'artistic' food you bring in brown sacks?"

Jeannie laughed. Roberta just stood there. Her eyes were on my coat and the look of distress that covered her face confused me.

I turned back to Bobby. "No, that's my aunt. She's artistic, too. Maybe I should share some of her creations with you. Looks like you never eat anything, String Bean."

"Wow!" Jeannie said. "Ph-red's getting tough. We may have to stop picking on him. Could get dangerous."

I folded the scarf and put it on the shelf next to my lunch. Then I unbuckled the belt and took off the coat.

"You gonna leave that precious piece of art in a locker all day?" Bobby asked. "Aren't you scared somebody'll steal it?"

"No," I said, hanging the belt on the hook in my locker, "but if anyone does, I'll remember who had the idea first."

"Hey, Roberta," Jeannie said. "Cat got your tongue?"

"She's probably just awestruck by the beauty of Ph-red's masterpiece," Bobby said.

Roberta glared at me. "Your mother didn't make that coat," she snapped. "People don't know how to make a coat like that by hand and, even if they did, they wouldn't bother."

"My mother does."

"You're putting us on," Roberta said.

"What's your problem, Roberta?" Jeannie asked. "Who cares whether her mother really made it or not? I suppose you think it's a great coat?"

Roberta shrugged. Then she walked quickly down the hall toward our homeroom.

I hung my coat over the belt and slammed my locker door as the late bell rang. Bobby and Jeannie and I ran behind Roberta.

At the end of third period, I got my lunch from my locker and went to the cafeteria with butterflies in my stomach. While I waited in the milk line, my eyes searched the tables for a familiar face. Any familiar face. As I paid for the milk, I saw Patricia and another girl sit down at a table right in front of me. Patricia's mouth was painted a bright pink today.

"Do it," I said to myself. "You have to do it." I took my

milk and practically ran to the table; I had to get there before I lost my nerve.

"Hi," I said. "Can I join you?"

"Sure," Patricia said. "How're you doing? You got your English homework done?"

"Yes." I sat across from Patricia and her friend.

"This clown's Colleen," Patricia said, jerking her thumb at a plump, lively-looking girl next to her.

"Hello," I said. "I'm Mary."

"What *is* the homework for today?" Patricia asked me. "You notice I almost never have it done?"

I laughed. "Yeah. I've noticed a couple of times."

The homework for English was an exercise on the use of commas and conjunctions as connectives to link main clauses. I'd worked hard on it Tuesday night; I didn't want to make an error if Mr. Dolsey called on me.

Walking to his class with Patricia, I tried to ignore the butterflies starting their uproar in my stomach all over again. They upset my stomach for nothing, though; Mr. Dolsey was absent. As I entered the room, a young woman with short kinky blond hair was sitting on his desk, painting her fingernails.

"I'm Miss Candlish," the young woman said when the bell rang. She finished the nail she was painting before she started calling the roll and she read the names from the sheet of paper without touching it. Then she maneuvered her copy of our grammar text into a position between her wrists, holding her wet fingernails out from the book. She let the book fall open on the desk and even turned the pages with her wrists!

"I understand you have exercises on page eighty-seven today," Miss Candlish said. She didn't say a word about

Mr. Dolsey's absence. I should have felt relief at not having to face him. Instead, I felt more nervous. Questions whirled around in my head the whole period. Why was he absent? Was he sick? If not, what was he doing? Why hadn't Mrs. Crider gotten in touch with me? What was going on?

Miss Candlish chatted away most of the hour. Every sentence we had in the grammar exercises reminded her of something she thought was "so interesting" or "just hilarious." Patricia was the first person Miss Candlish called on to read two main clauses and then link them with a comma and a conjunction. "Speeding drivers may admit guilt and pay a fine," Patricia read. "They may choose to appear in court and plead not guilty." Miss Candlish didn't get around to asking Patricia to link the two sentences until ten or fifteen minutes later. I guess she thought we'd be delighted to hear all the details of her first speeding ticket and appearance in court.

The class was a total waste of time.

I had the lamp on in the front room long after Aunt Louise and Uncle Mack went to bed Wednesday night. A week had passed since Mama's letter about her new job and the community center classes. I wrote her to say how happy and proud I felt. I underlined "proud" and drew a huge smiley face like the ones she always drew for me. At the end of the letter, I apologized for not sending congratulations sooner.

The biggest job of apologizing I had to do that night was to Cindy Lou. I wrote her a letter and then tore it up. After I tore up a second one, I went out to the kitchen and made a peanut butter sandwich. I wondered if I should outline the letter before I wrote it.

I got in bed with the peanut butter sandwich and thought about what Mrs. Swiggett taught us about considering your audience whenever you write anything. The tone, choice of words, and content must be appropriate for the intended reader. I giggled. I was planning this letter like a formal paper for English. For a grade. I tore out more paper from a notebook. Better stop making light of this and get down to serious business, I told myself. This *is* for a grade, Mary Fred, and you're probably going to fail.

Dear Cindy Lou,

Thank you for getting the coat out of the house and having it mailed to me. When I see you again and we have a long time for talking, maybe I can explain how your letters and what you did with the coat helped me when some things at school got so hard that I thought about coming home. I gave up that idea fast, though, and decided to show a few people here — myself included — that I'm not a quitter.

Today I wore my coat and held my head up high. Some kids hassled me. One girl, though — Roberta Thompson, the one I've written you about — surprised me. She's a ringleader, so she usually makes the most trouble. But she didn't ridicule the coat at all. Instead, she accused me of lying when I said my mother made it. You know what? I think she just might have been jealous of me.

I hope you're not still mad, but you've got a right to be. I did wrong. Even so, you wrote mighty strong words to me, Cindy Lou, saying I "don't take no pride" and don't have "common sense" for all my book learning. I do take pride in some things. I take pride in my schoolwork; I'm not ashamed to be a bookworm — I really want to go home to Dowell County someday and be a good teacher. I admit you're partly right, though; sometimes I spend too much time figuring out what's in books and not enough time learning about and caring about other things that matter. I think that's what you mean by "common sense."

In lots of ways, you're smarter than me, Cindy Lou. You've been faster than me in figuring out the most important things

135

to take pride in – like Mama, for example. I hope I never do anything else that would make Mama ashamed of me if she knew.

Bye for now. Hug Mama and Molly and June for me.

Your sister,
Mary Fred

P.S. When you see Mr. Hadley, you can tell him what I've said in this letter – or read it to him. I plan to get up my nerve to write him soon. I need to thank him for mailing the coat and tell him I'm sorry about being such a snot.

I put the letters for Mama and Cindy Lou on the shelf in the kitchen next to the corn-husk lady Molly and June sent me. Then I left a note to myself on the table, a reminder to ask Aunt Louise to put the letters out for the mail carrier in the morning.

Chapter 13

WHEN I WENT through the front door at school Thursday morning, the first person I saw was Norman. Even though he was a good distance down the hall and stood with his back to me, I recognized him right away. But the girl with him didn't look familiar until I came closer.

My heart fell. She was the same girl I'd seen him talking with in the hall before. Changing directions in order to avoid them, I stopped in midturn. Hadn't I decided to quit running from things?

I turned back around and walked right past them. As I did, I looked into the girl's face. I hadn't recognized her at first because the ponytail she'd worn when I first saw her was gone; now her long brown hair hung in waves over her shoulders. And she wasn't wearing her glasses, either. Her eyes were those big sky-blue ones like Daddy's and Mrs. Crider's — the beautiful color I'd always wished I had.

I don't think Norman even saw me. He was too busy laughing at something the girl had just said. I walked straight to my locker and then to homeroom. I wasn't going to go to the girls' room to cry and act like a baby. I wasn't going to waste one more minute thinking about Norman Garrett! He'd said he'd be seeing me — "soon, I hope." Well, he was mistaken. Obviously, he already *had* a girlfriend. I'd been dumb to hope he and that girl were just friends. And if he thought I wanted to join *Crabber Junior* and watch them talk and laugh while they walked to the paper's office every day, he was mistaken about that, too. Mattie was right: Norman was obnoxious.

Mr. Dolsey was absent again that afternoon. Miss Candlish was in the room, but she might as well have been absent, too. In the middle of one of her little stories about something that happened to her, a student came in and left a pink slip on Mr. Dolsey's desk. Miss Candlish handed the slip to me at the end of the hour.

In the hall, I read the note. "Please come to my office after school tomorrow," it said. The signature was "Gretchen Crider."

Late that afternoon while Aunt Louise and I were making supper, the phone rang. "Will you get that, honey?" she asked me, her hands covered in flour.

"Sure," I said and raced to the phone.

"Is Mary there?" a male voice asked when I picked it up.

I knew the voice right away. "This is Mary," I said. Even though I was surprised by his call, I managed to speak calmly. And to make my tone very cool.

"Oh, good!" Norman said, ignoring my tone or not even noticing it. "Hi, Mary!"

"What do you want?"

He caught on that time. The silence on the other end seemed to last forever. Finally, though, he went on. "I just got home from the *Crabber Junior* staff meeting and I was thinking of what we talked about yesterday."

138

"What?"

"About you joining the paper since you like to write."

I didn't answer.

"Well, would you like to?" Norman persisted. "Have you thought about it?"

I only hesitated half a second. "I'm not interested," I said. And then I hung up on him.

"It was for me," I said to Aunt Louise when I returned to the kitchen.

She didn't ask any questions.

Mr. and Mrs. Freeley invited Aunt Louise and Uncle Mack over to their half of the duplex for coffee and dessert Thursday night. They invited me, too, but I didn't want to go. I had a lot of homework and I didn't feel like being sociable, anyway; I felt like sitting alone and stewing about Norman and about what Mrs. Crider might say the next day.

"Just pound on the walls if you need us," Uncle Mack said as they went out the front door.

I started reading a chapter in my earth science book. Torture. I really don't care about the form, arrangement, and internal structure of rocks. I read two pages about three times each without a word of it sticking in my brain. I couldn't get my thoughts off what I'd done. I'd actually hung *up* on Norman! Well, he deserved it, I thought. Why'd he been so nice to me when all along he liked somebody else?

I closed my science book. Maybe he *did* like me, though. As a friend. Maybe I'd been wrong to act so snotty. Now what would I say when I ran into him at school? I probably wouldn't have to say anything, though; he'd avoid me. Well, that was all right—I didn't want to be "just friends" with Norman while that girl was his *girlfriend*. I couldn't handle the idea. Thinking about it was even more torturous than thinking about rocks. Sighing, I opened my book again.

I read the same two pages over for the fourth time and had just started worrying about Mrs. Crider when the ring of the phone startled me halfway out of my chair. Would that be Norman calling back? No way! I went out to the front room and answered the phone.

"Mary Fred?" a familiar voice said.

"Mama!"

"Hello, sweetheart."

"Mama! I can't believe it's you! Where are you?"

"I'm in Tyler, of course."

"No, I mean where are you . . . oh, gosh, Mama! You're at home. You got the phone, right? I *forgot* you were getting it."

"It was installed this afternoon late."

I shook my head and wondered if Mama's phone had been turned on the very minute I slammed this one down on Norman. "That's great!" I said to her. "How are you? How's your new job? What're you teaching over at the community center now? Tell me all about everything!"

"Honey, I'll write you all that, O.K.? You get my very first call, but I can't afford to run up a big bill."

"All right, but tell me a little! Do you like the people at the brass company?"

Mama didn't answer for a minute. "I can't talk about that stuff tonight," she finally said. "There's something else."

"Is anything wrong?"

"Yes. My first news on this phone's bad news. Mr. Hadley's only daughter's here with me. She come down from Michigan. Mary Fred, Mr. Hadley died Tuesday morning early."

"He *died*?"

"He died, honey. That heart specialist he seen put him in the hospital straight away – said he'd already had a minor stroke. Mr. Hadley's daughter come that very day."

"When?"

"Last Wednesday, day I started my new job. Her name's Charlotte and she's as fine a person as her father. She's been carrying me back and forth to my work for days on top of all her trips to the hospital."

"He's really dead?"

"Doctor had a big name for the coronary disease what killed him. All-out heart attack's what I call it. Struck him in the middle of the night Monday. He died Tuesday morning."

Why were tears filling my eyes? Was I crying because I felt sorry for Mama? She loved that old man so much. Mama kept on talking to me, but for a second I only heard Cindy Lou's voice: "He's good to our family." Then I remembered the things Cindy Lou wrote me: "He took up for you" and "He said Mr. Dolsey must not know talent when he sees it."

". . . folks from all over the county at that funeral," Mama was saying, her voice wavering. "He had so many friends."

I knew she was crying. "Oh, Mama, don't cry," I said. "The funeral's already over?"

"Had it today at noon. Don't seem possible he's gone."

What could I say to make her feel better? "I know how much you loved him and he . . . he was good to our family."

"His goodness didn't end when he died. Sweetheart, you won't believe what that man done. He must of knowed he couldn't make it much longer . . ." Mama stopped to blow her nose.

"What're you talking about?"

"Mr. Hadley had the title of that car of his changed over into *my* name! Did it several weeks ago and wrote and told

Charlotte should anything happen to him, that car belonged to me just outright. Ain't that something?"

"That's going to help you so much!"

"My, yes, but I don't hardly feel right about taking it. Charlotte says as how it's all been done up right and proper, though, and ain't a thing I can do but keep it. What's more, she says it'd probably fall apart if she tried to drive it all the way to Michigan." Mama laughed. "Well, it's a godsend to this family no matter how old it is," she said, her voice quieter.

"Have you got a license yet?"

"Charlotte's taking me to the test center tomorrow afternoon. Wish me luck, all right?"

"You'll pass."

"I think I will. Let me talk with Aunt Louise a bit."

"She's next door. Want me to run get her?"

"No, I guess not. I been on the phone too long, anyways. I better get off."

"You'll get a letter from me soon — probably Saturday. Aunt Louise mailed it this morning." Tears welled up in my eyes again. "Cindy Lou'll get one, too. Will you tell her I'm sorry I didn't send it sooner?"

"No need to worry over that, honey. You been good about writing us."

Maybe, I thought, wiping my eyes with my sleeve, but that letter was special. I wouldn't ever get to write to Mr. Hadley and now Cindy Lou wouldn't ever get to read that letter to him. He'd never know I was sorry for being what he called "proud" — the wrong kind of proud. But Cindy Lou said he took up for me. Maybe he understood.

"... you soon," Mama was saying.

"I miss you, Mama."

142

"And I miss you. You write us again when you got time. Bye, sweetheart."

"Bye, Mama."

I fell asleep thinking about Mama. About how alone she was with Daddy gone and now Mr. Hadley. I dreamed of blue crabs. In my dream, I was standing at the water's edge as the morning's new light spread slowly across a sandy beach, pushing back the darkness. I could see under the water, far out from the shore. The crabs were migrating. They moved past me, gliding toward the mouth of the bay. I peered into the water and stared at the red claw tips, the painted fingernails. All the crabs were sooks. Some traveled in groups. Many swam alone.

A strong cold wind blew my hair. As I felt the chill in the air, I saw the sooks swim more rapidly. I remembered the words Mrs. Swiggett had used to describe my mother: strength, dignity, courage. In the autumn cold, the sooks had no Jimmies to carry them. But they were strong. And they were moving, moving fast toward warmth and safety.

Chapter 14

I SAW MATTIE coming out of her house as I closed the door behind me Friday morning. "Hey, Mattie!" I yelled, running across the street.

"Hi, Mary! I haven't seen you for ages! What a *great* coat!"

"Thanks. My mama made it."

"Wow! It's super!" Mattie walked around me, eyeing the coat from all angles. "We better get going," she said, still nodding her head in approval of the coat.

It'd been a while since I'd walked with Mattie. I'd forgotten how fast she moves with those long legs. "Don't you have band practice this morning?" I asked, stretching my own legs to keep up with her.

"No. Mr. Carlson's in the hospital. He's real sick. Everybody's upset."

"I'm sorry." I thought about Mr. Hadley going to the hospital. And dying.

"We're going to have extra-long practices as soon as they find a substitute band teacher," Mattie said. "The concert's December Second; we've only got six weeks to get ready."

"Can I hear you play sometime?" I asked.

"Sure. Come over after school one day. If we don't have a sub yet, I'll be practicing at home." She turned toward me. "So, what've you been doing with yourself?"

While we walked the rest of the way to school, I told her about Roberta, Jeannie, and Bobby in the cafeteria and about wearing my coat the next day. I thought about my appointment with Mrs. Crider that afternoon, but I didn't want to say anything about Mr. Dolsey so I decided not to mention that. I just said casually that I'd been worried about my grades in English. As Mattie and I approached the school, I waited nervously for her to mention Norman seeing me with a bloody nose. Or the fact that I'd hung up on him the night before. She didn't, though; I should have known Norman wouldn't mention such things to his sister.

"Be sure and come over soon," she said in front of the building.

"I will."

When my last class ended, I went to the girls' room to wash my hands and comb my hair. Then I walked to my locker, got all the books I planned to take home, and put on my coat. After that, I hurried to Mrs. Crider's office. As I entered the room, she was standing behind her desk. Two other girls were already there. One of them was the girl I'd seen with Norman. The other was Roberta!

"Hello, Mary," Mrs. Crider said. "Please have a seat."

Three chairs faced her desk. The middle one was empty. I had to sit between them! Why were they there? What was Mrs. Crider doing?

"Mary, do you know either of these girls?" Mrs. Crider asked.

"Roberta's in my homeroom." I gazed intently at my feet.

"Then you know her. That's good." Mrs. Crider nodded toward the other girl. "This is Ann Sears. Ann, Mary Pratley's a good writer. You two should get to know one another."

Not if I can help it, I thought. I had no desire to know *her*.

"Ann writes poetry," Mrs. Crider said to me. "She's interested in starting a literary journal for our school."

Interested in spite of myself, I looked over at Ann. Behind her glasses, her big blue eyes smiled at me and she spoke with a warm, friendly voice: "Hi, Mary. I'm glad to meet you."

I didn't respond. Instead, I watched as Mrs. Crider searched through the stacks of papers on her desk. "A good writer," she'd called me. I relaxed a little. But why was Roberta there? And that girl, that Ann Whoever of Norman's?

"Ann's on the newspaper staff, too," Mrs. Crider continued, still flipping through things on her desk.

Maybe that's why she and Norman were talking in the hall! Maybe they were just discussing newspaper business. Oh, cool it, Mary Fred, I said to myself. Don't start getting your hopes up again. You're not going to think about Norman anymore. Remember?

"Would you like to help with the journal?" Ann asked me, turning in her chair. "I can't find many people who're interested in a literary magazine."

"I don't know," I said curtly. Then I looked over at her again. She was still smiling. Why was I being so rude? "Well, maybe so," I said in a friendlier voice. Why shouldn't I want to know Ann? What difference did it make if she was Norman's girlfriend? Norman was probably never going to speak to me again, anyway.

Mrs. Crider finally pulled out my English themes. "Your papers are basically good, Mary, especially the essay on the *Enterprise* and the report on Margaret Bourke-White, but

I think Mr. Dolsey's evaluations of the first two papers are valid. And —"

"*She's* got Mr. Dolsey, *too?*" Ann asked. Then she sucked in a huge breath of air and said, "Oh, I'm sorry! I interrupted."

Mrs. Crider went on. "The last paper *was* verbose, Mary. If you're serious about your plans, I'm sure you'll want to work hard to improve in the areas he's criticized."

My eyes wandered all around the office and then settled on Roberta. She was sitting perfectly still, staring out the window. Mrs. Crider's words hurt; I'd expected her to say all the papers were great. Well, maybe my writing wasn't as good as I thought it was. Mr. Dolsey said C and Mrs. Crider seemed to agree. Mrs. Swiggett gave me a B at the end of last year. And she constantly pointed out areas where I needed to improve.

"Mary?"

I looked up as Mrs. Crider passed the themes across the desk to me. "I'll go through the papers again and think about those things," I said.

She sat down. "Good. I admire Mr. Dolsey's high standards, but his grades are a bit harsh in my opinion; I don't think he gave enough credit to the strengths of your essays. With more effort I believe you may turn out some first-rate work."

"Thank you." She sounds just like Mrs. Swiggett, I thought. More effort. More effort. But I'd paid almost no attention to Mrs. Swiggett's criticism; I just memorized every word of her praise. In her letter, she said I have "enormous potential"; I'd thought that sounded really impressive. But maybe I should make out one of my little white cards for the word "potential"; it didn't mean the same as "already perfect."

Beside me, Roberta finally moved. She straightened out the sleeves of her sweater, the pink sweater she'd worn the first day of school and scrubbed in the bathroom. Mattie was wrong that she never wore the same thing twice.

"Do you want to take off your coat, Mary?" Mrs. Crider asked.

"No, ma'am," I said, although I knew I'd seem strange keeping it on; Roberta and Ann's coats hung from the backs of their chairs. But I needed mine for moral support.

"Well," Mrs. Crider said. But she didn't continue. She looked at me, then Ann, then Roberta. "Well," she said again. "I suppose each of you wonders why the others are here."

"Yes," said Ann.

Roberta was still staring out the window.

"You have a mutual problem," Mrs. Crider said. "Considering the speed with which stories spread in a school and the manner in which facts are often distorted, I decided to call you in together, put the facts before you, and clear the air of this matter once and for all."

Roberta still had not spoken, but she looked directly at Ann and then at me. She didn't scowl at me, either. Not that I cared.

"You've come to me individually with complaints—very serious complaints—about Mr. Dolsey," Mrs. Crider said. She left no time for us to react. She explained quickly that I'd been in last Friday to discuss what had happened to me two weeks before and said she wished I hadn't waited so long. The same day I came to her office, Mr. Dolsey made what Mrs. Crider called an "advance" toward Ann. Ann confided in her mother and came to Mrs. Crider with her parents the following Monday afternoon.

Mrs. Crider got out her cigarettes but didn't light one. "Tuesday morning, Roberta came to me to say Mr. Dolsey had been too familiar with her in his classroom on Monday afternoon. That may have happened at the exact time Ann and her parents were here with me." She shook her head. "I called Mr. Dolsey into this office from his second-period class Tuesday morning. I confronted him and suggested that he resign."

Tuesday morning! Later that same day I'd screamed, yelled, and sobbed my head off with Mr. Dolsey in the hall and in front of the school.

"What'd he say?" Ann asked, sitting up on the edge of her chair.

"He refused. But he seemed very agitated. He implied that Mary accused him falsely because she's angry about her grades. He referred to you, Ann, as 'a romantic, literary type with an excessive imagination.'" She turned to Roberta. "I'll be frank with you, Roberta. Mr. Dolsey characterizes you as a known troublemaker."

"That doesn't give him any right to paw me!"

Roberta's outburst startled me.

"It certainly doesn't. And I didn't say that his portrayal of you is accurate."

"He probably said more than that, didn't he?" Roberta asked, twisting one of her sleeves violently. "I know what he thinks of me!" Then, to my surprise, she burst into tears.

We all sat quietly for a minute.

Roberta pulled a tissue out of her purse. "Everybody says I'm a slut."

"Oh, Roberta," said Ann, "I never heard anybody say that."

"They do. One of my girlfriends told me. But it's not true." She wiped her eyes.

We all sat again without talking. Mr. Dolsey was right about Roberta making trouble, I thought. I felt angry at him, though, for what he'd said about me and Ann and for how he'd tried to deny what *three* people said by making us all out as liars to Mrs. Crider. Tuesday when he tried to talk to me, he never finished his sentence, but he referred to . . . what'd he call it? "This incident." I knew he didn't mean just the grades; he hadn't acted phony with me. But I didn't really blame myself for waiting so long to go to Mrs. Crider: I'd known he'd deny it all to her.

Roberta's crying was quieter.

"I understand that this is a very upsetting experience," Mrs. Crider said. "For all of you." She pulled a cigarette out of the pack and tapped it on her desk about fifty times. Then she sighed. "I'm trying hard to quit," she said. "I'm not supposed to smoke in front of students."

Ann smiled. "What are you going to do now?" she asked.

"When Mr. Dolsey refused to resign, I assumed I'd have to take this issue to the school board. However, he called me at home late Tuesday evening. He sounded upset and depressed and he asked to see me early the next morning. He came in Wednesday to submit his resignation."

"He resigned?" Ann asked. "Did he admit . . ."

"Not specifically. He simply said he's been under a great deal of pressure and that he felt this strain was affecting both his personal and professional lives."

"You mean that's it?" Roberta asked. "That's not fair!" Her gray eyes flashed. "He's just going to walk away without anything happening to him?"

"Something *has* happened to him," Mrs. Crider said. "He's had to give up the work to which he's devoted over twenty years. He's seeking other employment. He told me he'll also seek professional counseling for his personal problems. That will take time and effort. And it'll be expensive."

Roberta wadded her tissue into a ball in her fist. "That's

what he calls all this — 'personal problems'? If he didn't even admit —"

"The important thing for us now," Mrs. Crider said, "is that he's out of the classroom. I went to the superintendent on Wednesday afternoon. He called a special meeting of the school board for last night and I supported Mr. Dolsey's request that his resignation be accepted immediately. The school board did accept it."

"Why didn't you ask them to fire him?" Roberta asked.

"Roberta, he'll not be able to return to teaching — either by reapplying here or by asking for references should he wish to teach elsewhere — without showing that he has gotten professional help and benefited from it."

Mrs. Crider stopped talking and rubbed both of her eyes with the palms of her hands. "Excuse me," she said. "I'm a little tired this afternoon." She looked up again. "Before I went to the superintendent, I called the Cleveland school system and double-checked Mr. Dolsey's record. He's never caused trouble before and he's an undeniably successful teacher."

I suddenly felt sorry for her. How could she please every-body? If I got to be a teacher, I'd never try to work my way up; I wouldn't want Mrs. Crider's job.

". . . responsibility to protect my students," she was saying. "Mr. Dolsey's resignation takes care of that responsibility; my preference now is to give him a chance to resolve his problem."

"I guess that's fair," Ann said.

"Well, maybe," Roberta mumbled.

"I hope your parents will think so, too," Mrs. Crider said. "I wanted them to know the outcome of the school board meeting last night, so I've called them this afternoon."

"You called our parents?" Roberta asked. "My father?"

"Yes. I spoke to your father at his office. I was surprised to learn that he'd not been informed of this situation. And, Mary, your aunt was also uninformed."

I twisted about uncomfortably in my seat. The room suddenly felt so hot that I unbuckled my belt and opened the front of my coat.

Roberta yanked at a loose thread on her sweater sleeve and started crying again. I didn't understand. She pulled out another tissue and cried harder.

"Are you all right?" Mrs. Crider asked her.

"Yes, ma'am," Roberta sniffled.

Mrs. Crider waited until Roberta was calmer and then looked at all three of us. "The substitute you've had this week, Miss Candlish, has agreed to take your classes regularly. She signed a contract this morning."

"Oh, no!" Ann groaned.

I nodded at her in sympathy; she felt the same way I did about Miss Candlish!

"I've asked your parents to feel free to come in for a conference," Mrs. Crider said. "Should any of them have questions about the decision that's been reached, I'll at least try to help them understand my position and that of the school board."

She stood up behind her desk. "I've suggested to each of you separately that you not discuss these events outside of your homes and this office." For a moment her face was stern. "I hope you'll decide to respect my wishes." Then she smiled and walked over to stand beside us. "I'm pleased that you felt you could confide in me. If you have other problems in regard to this or should you simply need to talk, please come back. I'll try to help."

"Thank you," said Ann.

"I didn't mean to be rude, Mrs. Crider," Roberta said, gathering up her things. "I'm just still totally hacked off."

"With good reason." Mrs. Crider smiled at Roberta and sat back down at her desk.

Still shifting positions, I remained in my chair after Ann and Roberta left the room. I raised my eyes a second and then lowered them quickly. "I'm sorry I didn't take your advice," I blurted out.

"My advice?"

I kept my eyes on my knees. "About telling my aunt and uncle. I didn't want them to tell my mother and worry her. And I didn't know what they might do here at school. I guess I was afraid they'd make everything worse."

"I think you made a mistake in not trusting their good judgment, Mary."

"Yes, ma'am."

"Your aunt was very upset and concerned on the phone, but she was also warm and understanding. I'm sure you'll have no trouble at home." She paused a moment. "As a matter of fact, talking all of this through with your aunt and uncle might enable you to leave it behind you."

Maybe. Obviously, I hadn't left it behind me yet. Anger at Mr. Dolsey and regret at his loss churned around in my stomach, fighting with one another. I gazed out the window behind Mrs. Crider; for a second the sight of the chain link fence gave anger the advantage. But then I remembered Miss Candlish. And I thought of how Daddy always told us kids to "give credit where credit's due."

The sick queasiness in my stomach subsided and I sat up straight.

"Mrs. Crider, if Mr. Dolsey gets the counseling, will you give him a reference to teach again?"

"Yes, I will, Mary. I know that may not satisfy everyone and you may not understand."

"I do understand. Mr. Dolsey's one of the two best teachers I've ever had."

In the hall outside Mrs. Crider's office, Ann and Roberta were still talking. Ann was buttoning up her coat to leave, though. She tapped my arm as I started to walk past them.

"I'll talk to you soon about the literary journal," she said. "I can't stay longer now. My boyfriend's waiting for me."

"Oh," I said. Then I ventured, "I saw you with him in the hall the other day. He's on the paper staff, too, isn't he?"

Ann looked puzzled. "No. He doesn't go to school here. He's a sophomore. At the high school."

"Oh," I said again. I certainly wasn't making brilliant conversation. But I couldn't say "Hooray! That's great! He's not Norman!"

"I know your boyfriend," Roberta said to Ann. "It's Randy Forrest, isn't it? He's a friend of my brother. He's real cute."

"Thanks."

I ignored Roberta. "Ann, I . . .." I hesitated. "I might like to work on *Crabber Junior* instead of on the literary magazine."

She looked disappointed. "Why?"

"Oh, I don't know. I've never written short stories or poetry or anything literary. I write mostly essays; I'm better at expository writing — at least, I'm *trying* to be good at expository writing."

"Well, it's your decision. The newspaper staff needs help, too. I'll introduce you to their faculty advisor. I hope you change your mind, though. I could use a couple of hard workers to get the magazine going."

"Thanks for asking me. I'll think about it." I hated to

disappoint her. She was so nice and I hoped to be her friend. But I *did* want to be on the newspaper; I wanted to write what I wrote best, not just to be around Norman. I'd been interested in English and writing long before I ever even heard of Norman Garrett.

"I'll see you two later," Ann said to me and Roberta. She rushed off toward the back of the school.

I buckled Aunt Louise's belt around my waist and started for the front door, my head already working on another problem: what could I do about the way I'd messed up everything with Norman? Now he probably wouldn't want me on the paper staff.

As I pushed open the front door, I heard Roberta blow her nose behind me in the hallway.

"That's a nice coat," she said.

"What?" I turned around.

"I like your coat. Did your mother really make it?"

"I told you she did." I knew my voice sounded sullen. So what? Roberta didn't deserve friendliness. Who did she think she was?

"Well, it's right pretty." Roberta blew her nose again. "I made a fool of myself crying in there," she said.

Was I supposed to feel sorry for her?

"Listen," she said abruptly, "I'm sorry about Tuesday. In the cafeteria."

Did she expect me to say it was O.K.? Was she crazy?

"That kind of thing's why people say I'm a troublemaker," she said. "All my friends are smart alecks, too. The nice kids don't like me." She raised her voice. "But Mr. Dolsey doesn't have any right to talk about me to Mrs. Crider. I'm a rowdy, but . . ."

She threw her tissue into a wastebasket beside her in the hall.

She wasn't crying anymore. "Oh, well, at least he's making my reputation more glamorous – I'm not just a troublemaker, I'm a '*known* troublemaker.'" Suddenly she giggled. "Boy, I bet he hates me. You know what I did?"

"No."

"When he – isn't that funny, Mrs. Crider saying he was 'too familiar'? – put his dirty old hands on me, I jumped out of my chair and kicked him right on the shin!"

I couldn't believe she'd done that! Roberta's got spunk, though. Maybe she'd never run from anything in her whole life.

"You have to let people know they can't walk all over you," she said.

I fixed my gaze on her eyes and held it there. "That's right," I said. "You do."

We stood there awkwardly for a few seconds.

"That was really cruel, that stuff Jeannie and Bobby and I did in the cafeteria." Roberta looked down at her feet. "I wish I hadn't done that."

"I better get going," I said.

"My brother's coming to pick me up. I'll walk out with you so I can watch for him."

Outside, Roberta sat down on the front step. "See you on Monday, Mary."

Mary? *Roberta* was calling me Mary now? Well, that's what you wanted, I told myself; everybody calls you Mary and you can't stand to admit that you miss being called Mary Fred. Serves you right; from now on, you better figure out ahead of time what you really want.

I started walking away from Roberta, but then I turned around. "Why'd you cry so hard when Mrs. Crider said she'd talked to our folks?" I asked.

Roberta twisted her sleeve again. She was going to ruin that sweater. "My father'll blame me. He thinks exactly the same of me as Mr. Dolsey does." She shrugged her shoulders. "It's not my fault. Daddy's got a very low opinion of females."

Surprising myself, I sat down beside her. "I heard about your mother," I said.

"Yeah. So's the whole world."

Right away, I regretted mentioning her mother. Even though Roberta had brought up the topic of her family, she seemed embarrassed by my comment. She changed the subject quickly and started telling me about Ann Sears's boyfriend.

I just sat there, looking at her. She lived in that beautiful house and wore clothes like I'd always wanted. Even so, she'd just admitted that she was a smart aleck and that nice kids didn't like her. Suddenly I wondered if she acted like a smart aleck to cover up hurt and shame about her family.

Beside me, Roberta had changed the topic again. Now she was talking about the school play coming up in November.

"You've got a part?" I asked.

"Yes! And it's a really good one!"

While Roberta chattered about her part, my mind drifted again. Had her parents gotten a divorce? Did she ever see her mother? I knew how it hurt when one of your parents died. Wouldn't it hurt almost as much if one of them went away? Mattie had been right that Roberta's problems were no excuse for her being "such a snot." But maybe Roberta wanted to change. I felt amazed that she didn't really seem to hate me; she'd actually apologized to me! Maybe Roberta wasn't so bad after all.

When Roberta left with her brother, I started toward home. For a moment I amused myself by guessing the number of city blocks I'd pounded trying to figure out city people. Some of these people had problems I'd never even thought about. Mr. Dolsey did. So did Roberta. And now Aunt Louise and Uncle Mack had city problems walking right through their front door. Courtesy of Mary Fred Pratley.

All the way over in Kentucky, Mama had city problems troubling her, too, if Aunt Louise had phoned her as soon as she got Mrs. Crider's call. I walked slowly. Even though I was glad I'd talked with Roberta at school, I hadn't stayed so long on the steps just because of her. I'd stayed because I was scared to go home.

Chapter 15

STILL ABSORBED in my thoughts, I was almost in the yard before I noticed Uncle Mack's truck in the driveway. Had he come home sick? Or was he back earlier than usual because...?

I walked around to go in the side door. It was a beautiful fall day, the sun bright and the air crisp; if Uncle Mack wasn't sick in bed, he'd be on the porch.

He wasn't, though. As I approached the porch door, I heard loud, angry voices from the kitchen. Mrs. Crider was wrong that there'd be no trouble.

"A guy with a problem like that can't be allowed to continue earning his living as a teacher!" Uncle Mack said.

"He told Mrs. Crider he'd apply for a job as a technical writer at places like the shipyard and Fort Monroe and Busch Gardens," Aunt Louise said. "If he can't find something he's qualified for, he'll take what he can get. He's out of classrooms for the time being, so I don't see why you're so upset."

"*I'm* upset? You should've been on the other end of that phone, listening to yourself, when you called me."

"I'm not so disturbed about Mr. Dolsey as about—"

"Well, you should be! That woman's left it open for him to come back."

I knew I had to go in and talk with them. It was wrong to stand outside listening, but my feet wouldn't move.

". . . no right to make a decision like that behind our backs," Uncle Mack was saying.

"The whole school board made the decision. And Mrs. Crider said we can come in and discuss it with her if we want to."

"I'll be over to see her, you can count on it. And I don't understand the way you're taking up for this creep, Louise."

"I don't like what he did, either!" Aunt Louise's voice was shrill. "My blood boiled when Mrs. Crider told me about it. Imagine putting young girls like Mary Fred through such a thing! But I've had a chance to calm down some and I think Mrs. Crider probably knows best. After all, she knows the man. We don't."

"I know all I need to know about him!"

"You don't. He's done a terrible thing, but I don't reckon that's all there is to know about him."

"Somebody touches my niece, you think I want to know anything else about him?!" Uncle Mack was shouting. "Think I want to read his poetry?"

"Stop hollering at me! Mrs. Crider just means to help."

"I'm not interested in help for a guy like that!"

"Well, it's a good thing *somebody's* interested! Otherwise, he'll go on —"

"No, he won't! Not if he's kept away from kids. Let him come down to the shipyard with grown men and he won't go on getting funny ideas. We can handle him down there, I'll tell you that."

Outside, I felt miserable. I'd never heard my aunt and uncle

160

say a cross word to one another. Now they were having what Mama calls "a real go 'round." All because of me.

Aunt Louise raised her voice. "Sometimes you sound like one of those hard-hearted rednecks that —"

"Better that than one of those bleeding hearts that cry over every criminal! You want them running the streets?"

"Did I say such a thing? But Mr. Dolsey's not a murderer! He's a fine teacher who's gone off the track and messed up his life for a while. He has to stay out of the schools until he gets help, but it ain't necessary to have him tarred and feathered and railroaded out of town to accomplish that."

They didn't say anything for a minute or two. I put my hand on the handle to the porch's screen door. I had to go right in. Or go away. Or cough loudly so they'd know I was there. I couldn't let myself listen to their private conversation any longer.

When Aunt Louise spoke again, her voice was quieter. "Honey, what I'm most concerned about is Mary Fred."

"What on earth do you think I've been ranting and raving about?"

"Mr. Dolsey. You haven't said a single word about Mary Fred."

"Louise, you know good and well that's why I got so worked up. Maybe I..."

I coughed and opened the screen door. Uncle Mack heard me and walked quickly through the kitchen doorway and out onto the porch. Aunt Louise came out behind him.

"I'm glad you're home," Uncle Mack said to me. "We've got things to talk about. Get on over there and sit on the glider. I'm some kind of frustrated with you today."

I moved fast.

"Mack, what's wrong with you?" Aunt Louise asked.

"Mary Fred hasn't done anything." She sat down beside me.

Uncle Mack sat in the wicker chair next to the glider. He shook his finger at me. "Mary Fred, why'd you go through a thing like this and not tell me and Louise?"

Oh, boy. I felt sweat breaking out on my forehead.

"Mary Fred?"

"I should have told you," I said, avoiding Uncle Mack's eyes. "You could have helped me."

"Why didn't you, then, sweetheart?" Aunt Louise asked softly.

Keeping my eyes on the tile floor of the porch, I told them all the reasons I'd told myself at first and then told Mrs. Crider in her office. "Mrs. Crider said I'd made a mistake in not trusting your judgment," I said.

"Well, that woman's got good sense about something, at least," Uncle Mack said. He ran his hand through his hair and turned to me. "You're a special young lady in your own right, Mary Fred. I'd like you even if you weren't any kin of mine. But you are. You're my brother's child. I want to do right by you kids, but I need you to trust me."

"I do. I was just . . . just scared about everything."

"I know I can't take David's place," he said. "But I reckon I'm the closest thing you've got to a father these days." He leaned over and put his head in his hands. "Like I wrote your mama back in the spring, you kids are all I've got left of my brother."

I felt a tightening in my chest and tears came to my eyes.

When Uncle Mack looked up, his eyes were wet, too. "I need you to trust me," he said again. "Something like this — maybe you'd want to go to Louise first. Maybe it's easier talking to a woman about this kind of trouble. But when you got trouble, you come to one of us, all right?"

162

"I will."

He sighed. "I didn't handle all of this very well myself. Driving home after Louise called me, I kept thinking how you told us right in our kitchen that Dolsey was strange – 'creepy,' you called him – and that he made you and some of the other girls jittery. I should have checked into him right then."

"Don't take the blame on yourself, honey," Aunt Louise said. "Kids are always calling teachers 'strange' or 'weird' or 'creepy.' You didn't have any real reason for being suspicious."

"She's right," I said. "And I'm really sorry about not coming to you, Uncle Mack. I didn't think how you'd feel if I didn't seem to trust you."

After a minute, I turned in the glider and faced Aunt Louise. I had to ask the hard question. "Did you . . . did you call Mama after Mrs. Crider called you?"

"No, honey. I figured you'd want to tell your mother in your own way."

Boy, did I feel relieved! "Thank you, Aunt Louise. I *do* want to talk to Mama, but not until I see her again. I don't want to try to explain in a letter or on the phone. She'd worry too much."

Aunt Louise put her hand on my knee. "For now," she said, "don't agitate yourself anymore about all this. And as for not talking to your uncle, it might be best that Mack didn't know sooner, anyway. You should have heard how he carried on when he found out today. He gets way up there on his high horse when he's riled. If I had problems, I wouldn't want a bull like that bellowing around my school." She gave him a knowing smile.

Uncle Mack looked at me. "I admit I don't have much patience for a thing like this. Your aunt thinks I ought to keep my nose out now and not go making a hard time for Mrs. Crider. You think she's right?"

I paused before answering. "You're both right in a way. I don't blame you for being mad, Uncle Mack. I was so mad at first that I didn't know what to do with myself. I still am. Some."

"But?" Uncle Mack asked. "You're going to say 'but' and go on to tell me Louise is mainly right, aren't you?"

"Don't put her on the spot like that," Aunt Louise said.

"I want to know what she thinks," Uncle Mack said.

I started at the beginning and told them everything that had happened, even the stuff about Roberta, and everything I'd screamed at Mr. Dolsey on Tuesday. "I pitched a big fit on him," I said.

"Good for you!" Uncle Mack sat still a minute. "He did you dirt wrong and you turned around and did him a big favor."

"What?"

"You showed him plain as the light of day a cold, clear picture of himself. He called Mrs. Crider that night and did the right thing."

"I think Mrs. Crider's doing the right thing, too, Uncle Mack. I've thought it over a lot." I looked up at him. "I'll admit it: I feel the same way Aunt Louise does. I hope things work out for Mr. Dolsey. You should see the jerk we've got for English now. She's a complete weirdo."

Uncle Mack winked at Aunt Louise. "You go right ahead and side with your aunt," he said to me. "I'm not offended. After all, her ideas can't be completely stupid." He grinned. "A man like me wouldn't have married some dummy."

"Well, thank you," Aunt Louise said.

"Tell you what," he said. "Next time trouble comes down

164

the pike, I'll make a big effort, just for you, Mary Fred, to control my abominable temper and figure out the best way to help. I'll keep my cool."

"Now, that'd be something to see," Aunt Louise said. She got up and stood behind him, massaging his shoulders.

"Even rednecks can be cool," Uncle Mack said.

Over his head, Aunt Louise flashed me a broad smile.

I slept in late Saturday morning. When I got up, I found a hurriedly written note taped to the refrigerator. "Dear Mary Fred," it said. "Forgot to tell you I have doctor's appointment. Mack is going with me. See you later. Love, Aunt Louise."

I put on my oldest pair of jeans and one of Uncle Mack's work shirts. Then I got out the vacuum cleaner, some dust rags, the Ajax, and the window cleaner. I worked hard and fast, talking out loud the whole time. I always practice what I'm going to say in a crisis. And Monday I'd have a crisis to face: I had to find Norman at school. And I had to apologize.

When Aunt Louise and Uncle Mack came home early Saturday afternoon, Aunt Louise noticed the results of my work right away.

"Oh," she said, walking from room to room, "you've cleaned this place from one end to the other! Thanks, honey." She came over to the kitchen table and hugged me.

"Why'd you go to the doctor today?" I asked.

"Just for a checkup." She glanced at Uncle Mack.

Uncle Mack grabbed a can of beer and sat down next to me. "Your aunt Louise is in the family way."

"Oh!" I smiled at Aunt Louise. "That's great news!"

Aunt Louise took off her coat. She didn't say anything.

"Isn't it?"

"Of course. I'm just worried again."

"It'll be good this time," I said. "Your bad luck's over. Life's like that. Things go bad; then they always get better." I thought about Norman. "Usually," I added.

"You're profound today, Mary Fred." Uncle Mack reached over and mussed up my hair the way Mama does when she feels affectionate. "That's the best way to believe, though. Keeps you going."

"You don't have control over some things," Aunt Louise said. She sat down with us.

"Come on now, honey." Uncle Mack put his hand on her arm. "Worrying won't help a bit. The doctor says you're doing great so far." He turned to me. "She's four months along. That's farther than she was either time before. It's a good sign."

"There's nothing I can do if this pregnancy goes wrong," Aunt Louise said. "I feel helpless."

"Now stop your stewing right this minute," Uncle Mack said. "If Mary Fred and I say your bad luck's over, it's over. You just have to take extra special care of yourself, that's all."

"I know." Aunt Louise got up and poured a cup of coffee from the coffee maker. She drinks that stuff day and night.

"You could start by giving up coffee, honey. That's too much caffeine. I read somewhere that caffeine's as harmful as alcohol and nicotine to a developing fetus and —"

"*You're* going to talk to *me* about giving up things that aren't good for me?" Aunt Louise suddenly smiled. She put sugar in her coffee and tapped Uncle Mack's beer can with a fingernail. "Aren't you the world's biggest hypocrite?"

He pounded the table with the palm of his hand. "I'll put my money where my mouth is. I swear! Starting right this minute." He took his can and stood by the sink. "If I drink another beer before this kid's born, I'll pay for three months of diaper service. How's that? But you have to give up the coffee."

Aunt Louise's long fingers tightened on her cup.

Uncle Mack poured the beer down the drain. "You're right, Louise. I'm getting fat. It's not good for my heart, all this weight. Besides, I don't want to have my kid introduced to some fatso as his dad."

"*Her* dad." Aunt Louise winked at me. She walked to the sink and poured her coffee down the drain. "The bet's on!" She held out her hand to Uncle Mack.

Uncle Mack shook her hand hard. "It's a deal!" he said. Then he sat back down at the table. "I think we ought to do some celebrating. We've got an anniversary coming up Tuesday, Louise, so I'll take you two ladies out on the town Tuesday night. We'll go to the fish house and splurge."

"Now, there's an idea that perks me up," Aunt Louise said.

"And we've got to celebrate the baby, too," he said. "Maybe we ought to go up to Williamsburg next Saturday. You two interested?"

"I am," Aunt Louise said, sitting down again. "How about you, Mary Fred?"

"Sure! It's a great idea." It'd be even greater, I thought, if I could invite Mattie and Norman. My apology was going to have to be pretty fantastic, though, if Norman ever wanted anything to do with me again.

Aunt Louise leaned toward me. "A penny for your thoughts," she said.

I put my hand on her shoulder. "My thoughts: the baby's going to be fine," I said. "*She's* going to be magnificent!"

My aunt kissed me on the cheek. "You know, Mary Fred, I think you just might be right."

Chapter 16

SINCE I'D NEVER seen Norman walking to school, I decided he probably went in early to hang out in the paper's staff office. Monday morning, after I hung up my coat in my locker, I found *Crabber Junior*'s office and planted myself in the hall outside.

Leaning up against the wall, I practiced what I was going to say. I went over it again and again. I couldn't admit to Norman that I'd hung up on him because I was so jealous when I thought Ann Sears was his girlfriend. But I didn't want to make up some lie to tell him, either. So, I had to keep my apology short and simple. "I was in a very bad mood when you called," I'd say calmly. "My behavior was obnoxious and I sincerely hope you will accept my apology."

When Norman came out of the office, he wasn't alone. A tall, skinny man with wire-rimmed glasses walked beside him.

"Thank you, Mr. Kaufman," Norman said to the man.

I remembered the librarian telling me that Mr. Kaufman was the faculty advisor. When he turned away and started down the hall, I rushed right up to Norman and, naturally, forgot every word I'd planned to say.

"Norman," I said, "please don't walk away because I have to tell you some stuff and I know you're mad at me – you have every right to be because I was really rude after you'd been real nice to me –"

I looked up at Norman and couldn't read a single expression on his face. "– but I want to apologize because, see, the afternoon you called me about joining the paper staff, I was in a really bad mood because I'd been worrying about a –" Norman didn't look friendly at all. "– a lot of stuff like these problems I've had with –" He didn't look angry, either, though. "– with that girl Mattie and I were talking about the night Mattie knocked your papers off your bike – you know, Roberta, and –"

Oh, it was awful, but I decided the expression on Norman's face was *boredom*! "– and some other things, too, that've caused me trouble, the worst one being that I . . . I got worried about something I thought was one thing and it was actually something else or, anyway, not what I thought it was so –"

I looked down at the horrible red splotches spreading all over my arms like they do every time I get nervous. "– so I'm really sorry for acting like I did when I . . . I . . . hung up, since that was an awful thing to do but –" The splotches on my arms were turning purple! "– but if you're not too mad at me, I'd like to be on paper staff, but I don't want to do that if you don't want me to be around because –"

"If *that's* how you write," Norman said suddenly, "there's not much point in your being on *Crabber Junior*."

"What?"

"If you write with fifty million run-on sentences that never end and half of which don't make any sense, there's not much –"

The bell rang. Norman didn't finish his sentence. "We're going to be late," he said. He didn't move away, though.

Determined to get it all over with, I plunged ahead. "Well, if I get rid of my run-on sentences, what *do* you think about me being on *Crabber Junior* staff?"

"Get to your homerooms!" a teacher called to us from the other end of the hall.

"I think you should call me at home tonight and we'll talk about it." Norman walked away from me. "I might hang up on you, though," he said over his shoulder. "See you." He ran down the hall.

I walked rapidly to my homeroom. Norman hadn't said "soon, I hope" this time. But he hadn't told me to drop dead, either. Was he joking when he said he might hang up on me? Or was he being sarcastic? His tone was as hard to read as his facial expression. Did he really want me to call him tonight? What would I say? More scary, what would *he* say?

At the end of last period, I went by the band room, hoping I might see Mattie. The room was empty, so I hurried out of the school. I was lucky. She was just starting down the street as I crossed the front walk.

"No sub for band yet?" I called after her.

She waited for me. "We're getting one tomorrow. We'll have our first extra-long practice then — we'll probably be here until six o'clock most days from now on."

"How's your practicing coming?"

"Not so good. I've got one tiny solo part and every time I play it, I think about performing in front of all those people and I blow it."

"That's all right."

"What?"

"You're supposed to blow it. You don't want to get up there and start beating on it."

It was a corny joke, but Mattie cracked up.

"Can you play for me this afternoon?" I asked.

"Is another day O.K.?"

"Sure," I said, trying not to sound dejected.

"Listen, I do want you to come today. It's a *perfect* day for you to be there – I'm going to need moral support. But something's coming up, so I'm not going to practice this afternoon. I have to be prepared for this other thing. I'll tell you about it when we get home."

"Sounds mysterious," I said, feeling better.

"How's everything going with Roberta and her crowd?" Mattie asked. "You got them tamed now?"

How could I tell her about the latest chapter in the Roberta story without telling her about Mr. Dolsey? Mattie's the kind of person you can trust, but Mrs. Crider asked us not to talk about it around school. Mattie was definitely part of school. And she was Norman's sister, too. I couldn't take a chance on Norman hearing about all of that. I'd die of embarrassment.

"The strangest thing happened," I said. "I ran into Roberta in the hall the other day and, right out of the blue, she said she liked my coat." I told Mattie all of the rest of the conversation except the part about Mr. Dolsey. "What do you think?" I asked.

"Maybe she's got possibilities. Keep me posted. She could use some new friends. You know – high-quality people like me and you." Mattie laughed. "If you decide she's O.K., I'll be nice to her, too. If *I'm* nice to her, she'll definitely have it made! Her status will go *way* up!

We stopped in Mattie's yard. "I better tell Aunt Louise that I'll be at your house," I said.

"O.K. But hurry. We don't have long."

I ran home. In the kitchen, I dumped my books on the table

and told Aunt Louise I was going to Mattie's. Then I went to the bathroom to wash my face and comb my hair. Would I still be at Mattie's when Norman got home from school? I put on a *tiny* bit of Aunt Louise's lipstick. Drawing in my lips so she wouldn't notice the color, I rushed past the kitchen on my way out.

Mattie was waiting for me on her front stoop. "Keep your coat on and let's sit out here," she said.

I sat down beside her. "How come?"

"Norman'll be home soon. I can watch him coming down the street from here."

"*That's* the big mystery, watching for *Norman*?" What was going on? "I thought you didn't even like him. He's obnoxious, remember?"

Mattie grinned at me. "Don't you dare say a word about this, but I'm so nervous because Norman's bringing his friend Tom home today."

I kept my voice very casual. "Isn't it way too early for Norman to be back? Doesn't he have a paper staff meeting?"

"He's leaving early today. Wait'll you see Tom. He's absolutely gorgeous! He and Norman haven't been friends very long and I've never met Tom, but I've seen him at school. He's on the basketball team and . . ." She stopped and put her hand on her chest. "Oh, here they come! I can't stand it! My heart's going to fail!"

My heart wasn't exactly calm, either. Norman had asked me to call him tonight. He hadn't invited me to be sitting on his stoop when he came home with his friend.

Norman and Tom raced down the street on bicycles. In a few seconds, the bikes rattled across the sidewalk. Norman and his friend braked on the grass.

172

"Come on," Tom was saying, "you'd be the star of the team in no time."

The two boys got off the bikes. Tom had black hair and dark eyes. He wasn't as tall as Norman, but he had long legs like Norman and Mattie do.

"I'm not interested in being a star," Norman said as they crossed the yard. "I'm interested in other things. You're the only jock I even *like*."

"Think about it," Tom persisted.

"Jocks bore me," Norman said.

"Don't say no until you think about it some more."

As they stopped in front of the steps, Norman hit his friend playfully on the shoulder. "Call me about it tonight. Pressure me about it long enough and I just might hang up on you!" He glanced at me.

Tom looked totally perplexed. "Huh?" he said.

"Inside joke," Norman said. "Some people — you pressure them about joining something and they get *suu-per* annoyed!" He smiled at me. A really nice, big smile! "This is our friend, Mary Pratley," he said to Tom.

He wasn't going to give me the cold shoulder after all!

"Hello," I said to Tom.

"And that ugly thing," Norman said, nodding his head toward Mattie, "is reputed to be my sister."

"She's not as ugly as you," Tom said.

"Thank you, sir." Mattie stood up and made a mock bow.

I looked at her in admiration. She sure didn't *seem* nervous.

Tom balled up his fist and aimed a mock punch at Norman's chin. "Of course," he said, dancing around Norman like a boxer, "a person'd have to be UG-LY to look as bad as you, Garrett."

"Well!" Mattie pretended indignation. "Sounds to me like

'not nearly as ugly as Norman' isn't a very special category."

"Oh, I blew it, ma'am," Tom said. "I was trying to pay a compliment to your fair-haired beauty and I've insulted you instead. My apologies, my lady." This time, Tom bowed to Mattie, a low, sweeping bow, waving one arm out in front of him. In jeans, a torn sweatshirt, and old tennis shoes with frayed strings, he looked ridiculous.

Mattie giggled. She was charmed.

"Time to hit the refrigerator," Norman said to Tom. "I've got to get started on the paper route."

"Excuse us, ladies." Tom went up the steps behind Norman.

Norman held the door open for Tom, but he didn't follow him inside. "Mary," he said, "*if* you decide you want to work on the paper—"

"You're thinking about joining *Crabber Junior?*" Mattie asked me. "I didn't know that! Hey, that's super!"

Norman frowned at his sister. "I'm on the paper staff. How come you don't think *that's* super?"

"Because nothing *you* do impresses me."

"You're such a pain, Mattie," Norman said. Then he turned back to me. "Why don't we get together after school one day? Wednesday'd be good because the whole staff's there on Wednesdays. You could meet everybody and see our setup."

"I guess that'd be all right," I stammered. My heart was pounding like crazy. I wished I could act calm and witty the way Mattie did. "Should I meet you at the paper's office?"

"Sure." He glanced at Mattie's back. "I know you know where it is," he said and flashed me another smile as he went inside.

The second the door closed, Mattie grabbed my wrist and squeezed it tight. She put her hand over her heart again.

174

"Oh, I feel faint!" Suddenly she leaned forward, tucked her head under her legs, and flipped over into the yard. "I'm expiring from love," she panted and then stretched out and lay rigid as though she were dead.

I burst out laughing. "You're losing it, Mattie. You're really nuts, you know it?"

She didn't move.

I laughed again. Mattie was just about the nicest, most fun girl I'd ever met.

"Isn't he gorgeous?" Mattie balanced her body on her forearms and held her legs up in the air. "I mean gorgeous with a capital G!" she said as the legs swayed wildly.

"Yes. He's gorgeous. With a capital G." There was no harm in Mattie thinking we were talking about the same person.

As we finished up supper, I asked Aunt Louise and Uncle Mack if I could invite Mattie to go to Williamsburg on Saturday.

"Of course," Aunt Louise said.

I reached up to the shelf over the table and took down the corn-husk doll Molly and June made. Trying to appear engrossed in rearranging the ribbons around the waist, I asked, casually, "Could her brother go, too? If he wants to?"

"Sure thing," Uncle Mack said. "That Norman's a great kid. The more the merrier."

"I'll call right now and ask them." I went to the front room.

Mattie answered the phone. "Oh, great!" she said when I invited her. "I haven't been there for two years. Can we go to the blacksmith's shop? They shoe horses there and make horseshoes, and we could go to the candle-maker's shop, too, because that's fascinating. I love Williamsburg!"

I gripped the receiver tight and bit my bottom lip. "If your brother wants to go, too, it'd be all right with Aunt Louise and Uncle Mack."

"Yargies."

"What?"

"Yargies. That means 'yuck.' Taking Norman would be absolutely yargies, yuck, obnoxious."

"Oh," I said. But I recovered fast — I wasn't going to let her hear my disappointment. "That's fine. You come by yourself."

"It'd be obnoxious unless . . . unless . . . oh, I've just thought of the most amazing scheme, Mary, for — "

I interrupted her. "You can call me Mary Fred."

"Yeah? Terrific! I think that's such a cute name; I already told you that, didn't I? Anyway, it'd be worth taking Norman if . . . Listen to this. I'll ask Norman tonight if he wants to go. He'll say yes, I bet you, because he's nuts about Williamsburg, too, and, besides, he's got a crush on you — I can't believe how much he talked to you today — anyway, I'll tell him to talk to Tom tomorrow and see if *Tom* wants to go. Would that be all right with your aunt and uncle? Would there be room?"

I was losing her. She thought Norman had a crush on me!

"Mary Fred? How many would that be?"

"I don't know. Oh . . . six. It'd be six. Hold on."

I went to the kitchen. "Would there be room if Norman's friend Tom wanted to go, too?" I asked. "I'm sorry; I didn't know this would get so complicated, but Mattie wants to know if . . ." I stopped and held my breath.

Uncle Mack's eyebrows raised. "You're sorry, eh? You don't look too down in the dumps to me," he said. "You falling for the Garrett boy? Or this kid, Tom?"

176

Aunt Louise slapped his arm. "Mind your own business, Mack!"

He grinned. "You kids'll have to ride in the truck bed. It's twenty-five miles. Might get awful chilly back there, but they're all welcome to go."

"Thanks!"

I ran back to the phone. "It's O.K.," I said to Mattie.

"I'll have to call you back tomorrow night. If Norman cooperates, everything'll be great! But he'll probably just say he's going and that if I want Tom to go, I'll have to call him myself. It'll take me all night tonight to talk Norman into asking Tom when there's no good reason for him not to ask him, but I think he suspects I like Tom, so he'll want to make things tough for me. He really is obnoxious. Soooooo, if I can't get Norman to invite Tom, I'll have to call you back tomorrow so you can help me practice what I'm going to say when *I* call him and—"

I laughed. No wonder Norman's so quick to notice run-on sentences; he lives with a nonstop talker. "Slow down, Mattie," I said. "I can't keep up with you."

"Well, you got the general idea of the plan, right? I'll call you back tomorrow. Definitely," she said and we hung up.

Chapter 17

TUESDAY WAS a happy night. Aunt Louise and Uncle Mack dressed up to celebrate their anniversary. I put on the skirt and blouse they'd bought me.

Uncle Mack helped me into my coat. "This is awful pretty," he said. "And, by the way, it's mighty nice to see you wearing it every day." He turned toward the bedroom. "Hustle up, Louise!"

"Hold your horses!" Aunt Louise came into the kitchen wearing a rose-colored wool dress and black patent-leather heels.

Uncle Mack whistled. "Now there's a good-looking woman!"

I'd never seen a grown-up blush, but Aunt Louise did. Unexpectedly, I realized what a nice time they could have if they celebrated alone. "Listen," I said, "you haven't been anywhere without me since I came here. It's a special night. Why don't you go by yourselves? Mattie's supposed to call me. And I've got homework."

I could see Aunt Louise had doubts. "I don't like to leave you here alone at night. And you have to have supper, too."

"I can make a sandwich. I'll lock the doors. And, like

Uncle Mack said, I can knock on the walls here; the Freeleys would come if I needed them."

"You sure you want to stay home?" Aunt Louise asked.

"Yes. It'd be a real date for you two. Very romantic."

Amusement brightened her eyes. "Romantic? A fish house?"

"I think it sounds all right, honey." Uncle Mack gave her a hug. "Might be nice, taking you out on a date."

"Go on," I said. "But no beer. And no coffee. You're on your honor. I want to see you shake hands again on your deal."

With a dramatic display of vigorous hand-shaking, the two of them went out the back door. After they left, I made a tuna fish sandwich. The phone rang before I finished it. It was Mattie.

"You won't believe this!" she yelled into the phone. "Norman invited Tom! I don't even have to practice my speech for calling Tom myself. They're both going!"

"That's great!" She didn't know just how great I thought it was.

"Every time Norman's nice to me, I get suspicious. But he really likes Tom, so that's probably why he asked him."

"Probably," I agreed.

"We've got to get down to the important stuff here," she said. "What're you wearing Saturday?"

"I don't know."

"I want to wear something that accentuates what Tom called my 'fair-haired beauty.' I guess Mama's right that I don't look as tall in a skirt, but Tom's not shorter than me — he's not much taller, but thank goodness he's not *shorter*! So, maybe I should wear jeans because they're more comfortable. Would a skirt be dumb on the truck?"

Mattie and I discussed all the possibilities for clothing.

179

We concentrated for about ten minutes on this problem and then considered three different ways Mattie might wear her hair. After that, we hung up.

I had just started my homework when the phone rang again.

"Hi, Mary Fred," Mama said.

"Hi, Mama! I got your letter. You have your driver's license! All right! How's everybody?"

"Fine. I ought not to be on here again, but I got a letter from Mack this week and it's important, so I thought I'd talk to all of you a minute."

"You're having bad luck getting Aunt Louise and Uncle Mack," I said. "They almost never go anywhere at night, but they're out for dinner to celebrate their anniversary. Guess what? They've got big news. They're going to have a baby!"

"I know! Louise wrote me. I'm so pleased for them."

"What was Uncle Mack's letter about? Can I know? Or is it personal?"

Mama laughed. "Remember when you were writing letters to your aunt and uncle behind my back?"

I bit my lip. "Yes, ma'am."

"Well, we just might be writing behind your back, too. I'll probably let you in on our plans, though."

"Plans?"

"I'm putting your sister on to say hello first," Mama said.

Oh, gosh! My pulse speeded up.

"Hello, Mary Fred."

"Hi, Cindy Lou."

Silence.

I swallowed hard. "Did you get my letter?"

"Yes."

Silence again. How could she be so mean? Wasn't she going to say anything?

"What'd you think?" I asked.

"It's a real good letter. I think you'll make a great English teacher."

"Cindy Lou, that's not what I mean! Why aren't you saying anything about what I wrote? Because Mama can hear?"

"Partly."

"What I want to know is, how good do you think I could be as a . . . as a sister?"

"You'll do."

"That's all? You're still mad at me?"

"Middlin'."

I'm making a little progress, I thought; "middlin'" mad's way less mad than "hopping mad" or "fighting mad."

"Mama's getting back on now," Cindy Lou said. "Bye."

"Bye, Cindy Lou." I grinned. "Middlin' mad" might be an improvement over "hopping mad," but it wasn't nearly as good as "not mad at all anymore." Cindy Lou had just given me a C on that letter. Well, I didn't deserve to be let off easy.

"Now, Mary Fred," Mama said, "tell me what you've been up to."

"Since my last letter to you, I've been thinking about joining the newspaper staff. I just met a girl who works on the paper and there's this boy who asked me —"

"Norman across the street?"

"What?" How did she know about Norman?

"Louise wrote as how he writes for the school paper and delivers papers in the neighborhood, too. She says he's an awful nice boy and she thinks you got a huge crush on him."

"Why's she think that?" I was glad Mama couldn't see me blushing.

"Louise's a smart woman. Never misses a trick."

I laughed. "She's so nice, Mama. She's . . . she's almost as nice as you."

"Of course! Mack and your father had very good taste in women."

"It's your turn to tell me what you've been up to," I said. "What're all these plans everybody's making behind my back?"

"They're about Thanksgiving. Louise and Mack'll head their truck this way, so if you're wanting to see us next month, all you have to do is climb in."

"Is that *definite*? Are you *sure*?" I jumped up from the sofa.

"According to the letter what just come from Mack."

"That's great!" I almost pulled the phone off the table. "I can't wait!"

"I think Mack and Louise are anxious, too," Mama said. "You know, I believe they get downright homesick some days."

I knew they did. They loved the Virginia coast, but they missed home. Uncle Mack told me that if he'd been born and raised here on Hampton Roads, he'd have salt water in his blood; he said he'd have made a crack waterman. But the way things are, his blood's full of the Kentucky hills instead of salt water.

"Uncle Mack says he's going to have to go back to Kentucky someday," I said to Mama.

"Reckon he will. Don't know that I could ever leave these hills myself. They're home."

I felt the same. When I became a teacher, I knew I'd head straight back to Kentucky. But I loved the city here and the rivers and Hampton Roads and the bay. I wished Mama and my sisters could share them all with me.

"I better get off this phone now," Mama said. "We'll be seeing you soon. Ain't long 'til Thanksgiving."

"I'll wear my coat."

"I should hope so! Lord, it'll be cold here by then!"

"No, I mean I'll be wearing it because . . . Oh, mama, I've got so much to tell you! I'll explain about the coat when I get home, O.K.? And lots of other things, too."

"All right, sweetheart. I can't wait to see you."

I smacked a loud kiss into the receiver. "You're special, Mama," I said.

"Well, you're not so bad yourself, Mary Fred Pratley. Just don't get too excited about the trip, you hear?"

"Yes, ma'am. Bye, Mama."

I didn't follow Mama's advice. I was so excited, I couldn't seem to settle down that night. While Aunt Louise and Uncle Mack were getting ready for bed, I got some scissors and cut out Norman's column from *Crabber Junior*. I wrote a short letter to Cindy Lou, enclosed the article so she could flip out over the gorgeous picture of Norman, and wrote just enough about him to get her curiosity going good. Then I addressed an envelope and stamped it. Cindy Lou loves getting mail.

After I put the letter on the shelf in the kitchen, I looked out the little windowpane in the front door and saw that the light was on across the street in Mattie's bedroom. She was probably still changing outfits and combing her hair into different styles, getting ready for Williamsburg four days in advance! I sorted through all my stuff in the front room closet; I had to figure out what *I* was going to wear to school the next morning. I'd be going with Norman to meet the *Crabber Junior* staff! I chose my best jeans and Cindy Lou's good sweater. Holding the sweater up to the light, I admired Aunt Louise's work: not a single trace remained of the stain from my nosebleed.

Folding the jeans and sweater neatly, I laid them out over the back of a chair in front of the window. Then I pulled out the sofa bed, arranged my sheets and blanket, and put on my pajamas. I didn't feel the slightest bit sleepy, though. I picked up one of Aunt Louise's magazines about knitting from the table beside the bed, propped myself up on pillows, and flipped through it. Near the front, I saw a picture of a sweater that looked just like the one Aunt Louise was making for Uncle Mack. Was that it? Skimming directions that I didn't understand, I turned over to the back pages of the magazine where the directions were continued. In the margins of one page were notes in pencil. Aunt Louise's handwriting. This *was* the sweater. I wondered if I could . . .

I jumped out of bed, tiptoed to the kitchen and stood quietly. I heard voices from the bedroom. Good. They were still awake. I went to their door and tapped on it.

"Aunt Louise," I called, "are you dressed? Can I talk to you for a minute?"

She came out of the bedroom in her bathrobe. "Is something wrong?" she asked.

"No." I motioned for her to come to the kitchen. I didn't want Uncle Mack to hear me.

In the kitchen, I whispered. "Can you teach me to knit?" I asked. "Can I make four sweaters for Christmas presents? One for Mama and one for Cindy Lou and one for Molly and —"

"Goodness, honey! That's a lovely idea, but . . ." Aunt Louise lowered her voice. "I've been working on that sweater for Mack 'most all day long for over two weeks and I've still got a long way to go. You couldn't learn to knit and then do four sweaters in just a few weeks, sweetheart."

"You're sure?"

"I'm positive. But you don't need to look so hangdog. If I help you, I think you could make scarves or mittens in time. Would you settle for that?"

"Yes!"

"We'll really have to get cracking. I'll start teaching you tomorrow night."

"Oh, thanks, Aunt Louise!"

She tweaked my cheek. "You get to bed now."

I got in bed and turned off the light, but I couldn't sleep. I was too excited about going to the newspaper staff meeting the next afternoon with Norman. And about going to Williamsburg on Saturday with my new friends. And going home to Kentucky for Thanksgiving. And making scarves or mittens for Christmas. And Aunt Louise and Uncle Mack's baby.

I turned the light back on and got one of my notebooks from the front closet. In bed again, I wrote a letter to Mrs. Swiggett. I liked writing to her; I wanted to keep in touch so she'd know that I was always trying to live up to her faith in me. Mrs. Swiggett's one of those people like Mama and Uncle Mack and Aunt Louise: you can't afford to let them down.

When I finished the letter, I put my notebook back in the closet. I stood by the closet door for a minute, running my hand across the rough, strong fibers of my coat. If I could learn to knit, maybe I could learn to weave someday, too. Mama and Cindy Lou would teach me. I'd make a tiny little coat for Aunt Louise and Uncle Mack's baby. A two-year-old's size!

I pulled the coat off the hanger, stretched out the arms, and waltzed around the bed with it. "What do you think of that idea, Mama?" I asked. I gave the coat a big hug and laid it out over the back of the chair with my clothes for the next day.

Back in bed, I thought for a long time about Mama's voice on the phone, cautious but happy. Mama had her hopes up high; I knew she did. And so did I. Warm and sleepy, I pulled the covers up snugly under my chin. Through the window, the lights of a Virginia street fell across the bright, cheerful colors of my Kentucky coat.